THE CURE

Robert Stetson

ISBN-10:   1480214582
ISBN-13: 978-1480214583

By   Robert J Stetson

Preface

The Cure machine is the exact opposite of an MRI (**M**agnetic **R**esonance **I**mager). The inventor, Gill actually creates an MRE (**M**agnetic **R**esonance **E**xciter) that he calls "The Cure".

Just as the imager detects the frequency of bacteria, the exciter bombards the bacteria destroys the source of the disease.

Governments are threatened by the increased cost of Social Security due to increased longevity. Medical interests are threatened economically because they lose the profit from treating the diseases.

Even the criminal underground becomes involved.

This is the story of the socioeconomic impact of The Cure.

This is how the inventor, Gill uses clever schemes to identify and overcome his opponents who are hell bent on killing him to stop The Cure machine from becoming a reality.

Travel from the mercenary attacks on his life, to his marriage, a wedding turned bizarre. This is the sometimes humorous, sometimes tragic step by step action packed story of how Gill turns the tables and creates a brave new world.

Introduction

American Cancer Society statistics for cancer alone in 2012 are projected to be 577,190 deaths and 1,638,910 new cases. If we estimate that the new case level is unchanged, then the cure rate is only 64.8%.

What would happen if a machine could cure not just all cancer, but all viral and bacterial diseases as well with 100% success?

What would that do to the medical, pharmaceutical, insurance and hospitalization industries?

What would that do to the overall economy and what would be the reaction?

This story explores the miracle of "The Cure", the inevitable greed, the resulting geopolitical consequences, and the final outcome.

CONTENTS

Robert Stetson

Chapter 1 Gill's Dream

My name is Doctor Professor Gilbert Bennett and I hail from the small town of Crawdad Alabama where I grew up a poor black boy in a sea of poor black people.

My mother worked from sunup to sundown just to pay for the simple things like food and sneakers.

I remember my mother saying, "Son, it doesn't matter if you're rich or poor. When you were born and I saw your sweet little face, I knew you were born to greatness.

"Don't matter what others think as long as you believe in yourself and always make yourself be proud."

Mom always did talk that way. I love her so much.

As a boy, I grew up loving science. While the other boys were playing stickball, I would sit under a tree reading a book.

My dream, even at the time, was to make a major difference in the destiny of humanity.

I naturally went on to MIT's electrical engineering school on a special scholarship. Then I rounded out my education with a degree from Harvard Medical School where I attended on a student loan. Yes, I just seem to have a talent for anything technical or biological.

Later on as I became older, I often found the time to spend with Zelda. Zelda was a special lady with special qualities.

It's only natural that I would ask Zelda to marry me and, being the natural thing to do, Zelda said, "Yes."

People who know me have come to call me Dr. Gill. Zelda was loved by just about everybody. Zelda made a wonderful wife and made my life a heaven on earth.

I now recall how my lovely wife Zelda was working at getting an education so she could become successful too.

We shared a desire to make a contribution to humanity. It was just one of the many things we shared in common.

I promised her that things would be alright as long as she focused on the goal and worked real hard. Then the terrible news came regarding her malignancy.

She lasted nine months after the diagnosis. I remember that I had promised her a miracle, but it just never came in time.

One way or the other, I just always seem to have money, lots of money, but it could never buy Zelda a second chance at life. The wealth I gained is an outgrowth of my poverty where I learned to control my spending and adopt a meager lifestyle.

You would never know I am so financially enriched because I never live that way. My needs are humble and I seem to care only for the people in my life and my goals. Money seems of little importance to me.

No one ever seems to catch a moment when there is anything spectacular about me. I walk the halls of the University, when I'm not teaching a class, in my old khaki pants. My sweater usually has a couple of holes in it and my hair will be in disarray. I am innocently unaware of my appearance and just never seem to care. My mind always seems to be elsewhere.

As I leave the house it's raining hard. The brisk wind is whipping my clothes and the umbrella serves no purpose other than to give me something to struggle with as I try to get my car door open.

I fold the umbrella and place it on the floor in front of the passenger seat.

Although the wind has totally rearranged my hair, it looks no different after the ordeal.

As luck would have it, today is a special day. I am working late in the Magnetic Imaging Lab and in this special moment, it occurs to me that the Magnetic Resonance Imaging machine is simply a generic broadband electron excitement medium designed to get molecules to vibrate at their resonant frequency, so I can map the body layer by layer.

I am wondering why it can't work in reverse and excite only those molecules I want by focusing a narrow band of magnetic waves on the object I wish to effect.

Having mapped the tumor and using its resonant frequency to display it, why can't I inject those resonant frequencies unique to the offending molecules and destroy only those, leaving all the molecules around them unscathed?

As I walk to my car in the brisk autumn wind, I decide not to involve any understudies in this work because competition is fierce in health research and I want to be the first to refine this miraculous solution.

The more I refine my work, the more I am coming to realize that it can work for anything that has a unique fundamental frequency, not just cancer. My excitement grows and I work feverishly into the night.

The news of my mother's passing found me having breakfast in my humble little house near the university. I wept openly. First I mourned the death of my lovely wife Zelda, and now the death of my mom. Death is forever working to destroy people. I can't stop remembering many of my mother's words of wisdom.

As I head out for work, the memory of my mother and her haunting words remind me, "It isn't what he has that makes a man great, Gill, but what he is. You are nothing more than the value of your word. Always keep that sacred."

Now I look at the work I am doing and see the fruits of the promise I made to Zelda. Most men would have taken days off to mourn the loss of their loved ones, but I am on a mission and the bad news spurs me on.

I have created a machine that puts an end to the evil that death and disease brings. I smile, but then, there is the tear that betrays my joy, for my joy comes too late.

Perhaps it's the full body sized chamber that gives my secret project away to his colleagues.

The other Professors constantly stop me in the hall between classes to ask, "Gill, what is that thing you're working on in the lab?"

I just smile and tell of the possibility of sterilizing the entire body surface prior to surgery without hurting the patient.

They walk away shaking their head in disbelief.

I am working late into the night, most nights. With nowhere to go and no one waiting for me at home, I have nothing left but my work.

I am on my way to the local veterinary clinic to speak with Dr Morgan about some of the animal patients there. Some of the dogs in Dr Morgan's care have been diagnosed with terminal cancer and they are there to be put down.

I propose a standing offer to buy any of the dogs from their owners with the understanding that the dogs will be returned to them after an experimental treatment in the event that it cures them. Being desperate, some of the owners are consenting.

My only fee is the contract requiring the owners not to divulge the means by which the animals are being treated.

Today I am taking a black Labrador retriever named Muffin back to the lab for treatment. I sit on the sofa in the lab and Muffin lies with his head on my lap.

The dog is clearly affectionate and looks to be in great pain. I administer an anesthesia, knocking the dog out and place it in the chamber connected to the MRI machine.

I turn on the power and start the scan. The cancer is wide spread. The dog clearly is near the end of his life.

The sixty-four slice magnetic imaging machine labors away in the corner of the lab and the computer connected to the data element of the machine is busy processing and cataloging the resonant frequencies of the many organic objects.

Now I have to manually correlate the data in the finite element analysis program. It's tedious work.

I start displaying the various key components that are foreign to the animal species. The readings from a healthy male black lab act as a reference. The machine finally displays only the three dimensional image of the malignancy in the laser imager.

The fog that is the cancer is ugly, large and well distributed as it is displayed in three dimensions. The striking image forms in the cloud chamber that I use as a visual display.

I transplant the resonant topography of the malignancy to the MRE or "Magnetic Resonance Exciter" and then press the start key.

The MRE springs to life and bombards the dog with high energy radio waves at a very specific frequency.

Special "Q" filters prevent the emission of resonant frequencies that may inadvertently damage other tissues.

The dog's unconscious body twitches as it is scanned. The scanner finishes and the dog lies still.

The image in the fog chamber melts away, slowly revealing a crystal clear video cube.

I check for a pulse and then check the blood and find that the remnant toxin levels are too high, so I perform a transfusion and wonder if I might have killed my new friend.

I sit by the dog bed and try to sleep, but my concern is not letting me. The sun comes up and the dog is still laying still, the rays of sunshine from the skylight splash across Muffin's black fury body.

I reach over and tousle the dog's fur affectionately. I can't help myself. I wipe away a tear and proceed to check for a heartbeat. Muffin still has a faint heartbeat and is breathing in shallow breaths.

I rise up out of my chair and go into the adjoining room where I start to make a cup of coffee. "How can I be so crazy as to think I can stem the tide of certain death?" I wonder.

I am feeling somewhat weak from not eating and I haven't slept in 20 hours.

Then there is a strange noise as the coffee perks. I check the old coffee pot and realize that it's not the pot.

I rush to the doorway of the lab and see Muffin standing upright with his tail wagging.

Muffin's tongue is hanging out. He has a big doggy smile and Muffin's eyes are clear and bright.

I rush to the dog's side and give Muffin a big hug. Muffin licks my face. For the first time, I can see the fire of life in the eyes of the old dog where there had only been pain.

Muffin eats well and especially likes the big beef bone. He chews on it vigorously.

I return the frisky dog to the Veterinarian who is simply amazed, but agrees not to ask any questions. The dog is returned to its owner who rejoices. Muffin is healthy now, and for now, my secret is safe from the scientific community.

It's been a year of hard work and I am still working with dogs. I am managing to cure a number of dog maladies, such as cancer, distemper, and other diseases by targeting the specific molecules, viruses or bacteria that cause the malady.

Cures are immediate and the symptoms are gone within 12 hours of the procedure. The deadly components of malignancies are converted to toxins which the body eliminates within three to thirty days.

In more severe cases, a blood transfusion is needed immediately after to prevent death from toxic shock. Permanently damaged tissues heal. While damaged organs do not regain their full functionality at least they do stop their deterioration.

Physical abnormalities are not cured because there is no invasive cause to be eliminated.

I decide not to patent the machine and the process because patenting requires full disclosure. I am relying on the trade secret approach to protecting my technology.

Of necessity I have turned to writing various medical and engineering papers on each aspect of the treatment without disclosing the particulars of the design.

By now, Dr Morgan, the Vet is exuberant. He says, "Gill, you old dog. I can see a Nobel Prize in your future."

I just smile, nod, and then say, "Thank you."

I look down at the latest project; a small dog named "Rags." The name seems so appropriate because the long fur is disheveled and unkempt.

It's a bitter sweet thing to watch the pain and suffering of innocent creatures give way to the cure.

The time has come to get back to the lab and another long night of work.

Being a brisk winter day I decide to push the automatic starter remote control in my pocket to warm up my car while before I have to venture out.

The car explodes in a ball of flame.

I sit trembling for a while and then I go to dial 911 on my cell phone and notice a Police car pulling up to the scene.

The Police were apparently passing by and saw the incident. They take a detailed report. Then, they tape off the crime scene area.

The two Officers seem to be smiling broadly. It strikes me as odd under the circumstances.

The Fire Department is on the scene and put out the fire quickly and with a smile as well.

Dr Morgan and I are interviewed at length, warned not to discuss the incident with anyone until the investigation is completed and released.

I am told that a Detective may be at my house in the morning to take further information.

After a night of fitful sleep, I decide to call the Police Station to inquire as to what they found out. They say there is no record of any incident the night before involving a car bomb.

I dress frantically and make a trip over to Dr Morgan's clinic. The parking lot is clean. There is no wreckage and there are no burn marks where there ball of fire erupted yesterday and most disturbing of all, there is no clinic.

Dr Morgan is gone as though he never existed. The building has no sign above the door. I look all around inside peering through the windows and find it empty. There are swirls of soap on the inside of all the glass and a for lease sign in the window.

I look around and find no evidence that anything ever happened here yesterday, but for a small shred of yellow plastic crime scene tape overlooked by the cleaning crew.

I stand there in disbelief and stare at the small yellow remnant in my hand bearing testimony to the incident I remember so vividly.

Why would so many people work together in an effort to cover up an attempt on my life, I mused. Where is Dr, Morgan and where are all the animals he cared for?

I have no time to dwell on the incident last night. I put Rags in the care of my staff and nervously pack my bags for a flight to Reno Nevada where the AMA is meeting.

I am scheduled to speak at the "Conference on Corrective Medicine" and I have my slide show neatly arranged on CD for the dissertation. The slides include my research results along with some technical information regarding the engineering aspects of the MRE.

My flight leaves in an hour and I am running a little late.

The limo arrives to transport me to the airport and I step inside with my bag.

A man is seated across from me in the plush Limousine interior and begins to speak with a harsh demeanor. He says, "Hello, Doctor Bennett I presume?

Care for a beverage or a Wall Street Journal?"

The man is stern, each word forced, as though he is just robotically speaking to fill some verbal requirement for initiating contact.

Robert Stetson

I look back at him and feel somewhat ill at ease. The greeting isn't a friendly one judging by the tone.

My suit is a bit rumpled and I begin to fidget.

My mouth opens and in a surprisingly weak voice I say, "Do I know you?" I pull out a handkerchief and wipe the perspiration from my brow.

The stranger ignores my question and says, "I have no qualms about killing you right here. It makes no difference to me, but I am told to try and do this quietly.

"You're on your way to deliver an in depth talk on some kind of machine to some group of people. I could care less what it's about.

"Listen closely, Dr Bennett. If you don't reconsider your position, you won't arrive there alive. Turn around. Cancel your talk."

At this time the car stops for a red light and the stranger, sporting a big smile, abruptly opens the door and exits the Limo. He slams the door and the light turns green.

My journey to the airport continues.

The limo pulls up in front of the airline terminal and I exit the limo lugging my bag which is heavy with slides and papers.

I make it a point to go straight to Airport Security and report the threat on my life.

I am greeted by Trooper Barney who listens with a great deal of interest to the entire story. "I'll get you safely on that airplane, Dr. Bennett." the Trooper assures him and then says, "You don't give us much to go on.

"There isn't anything we can do, and if there is a problem we will have to deal with it when it happens."

I reflect on the situation and say, "Maybe I shouldn't have wasted so much time reporting everything."

"Here, jump on board my security cart." The Trooper says. They arrive at Airport security.

It seems to be moving slower than usual and even though I have Trooper Barney paving the way through the security process, I find it unusually thorough.

Although the trip to the boarding area is swift on board the security cart, on arrival I am too late to board.

Trooper Barney shrugs and nods in the direction of two men standing nearby. They look as though they could be US Marshals waiting to respond to any situation that arises. It's as though they thought that there might be an incident, or maybe that I might be an unstable person. They obviously would have checked me out and verified that I am indeed a Professor at the local University.

The security cart slides quietly away.

I start walking down the concourse hoping to arrange another flight.

There is a terrible explosion and the glass on the tarmac side of the building shatters. People start to scream and scatter. I look over at the runway and see my airplane split open and in flames. Five more minutes and I would have been on that flight. My knees start to buckle and I have to sit down for a minute.

I tremble, working to convince myself that this is a coincidence. It occurs to me that the threatening stranger created the delay. When I stopped to report the incident rather than rush to catch my plane, it made me miss my flight. His death threat was largely responsible for saving my life.

After booking another flight, I am on my way to the conference where I will most certainly get the medical community to rethink their position on the lifesaving value inherent in my machine.

I ease myself down in the large and comfortable first class seat and I am determined to enjoy the flight.

Prior to leaving for the conference the AMA refused to proceed with clinical trials to evaluate the MRE procedure in humans saying it's far too dangerous to consider even if it does appear to work. I can't begin to imagine what the problem could be.

The test results have been spectacular with no adverse effects. Why are clinically unproven new drugs denied to people who are certainly going to die anyway?

I decide that in spite of all the stress, I should to try and get a nap.

My flight touches down in Reno, Nevada and I gather my luggage along with the presentation material.

As I step out onto the curb the air is still and the sun is intense. Today is unseasonably hot, even for this town.

A taxi pulls up to the curb, the driver loads my baggage in the trunk and then he says, "Where to, buddy?"

"Take me to the Airport Hotel. It's a real scorcher here today, isn't it?" I say trying to make small talk.

The driver ignores me and I am somewhat glad after feeling regret at trying to start a conversation with the stranger.

Having napped on the plane from sheer exhaustion, I do feel a lot better now. I actually sprint to the Hotel Lobby.

The hotel check in counter is quiet and I have to wait for a clerk to notice me standing there.

Finally one comes from the back room and asks, "Good evening, sir. Welcome to the Airport Hotel. Do you have a reservation?"

I nod and pull out my wallet saying, "Yes, I am Dr. Gill Bennett."

The clerk looks at me in disbelief and says, "Your room was given away just an hour ago when we heard of your untimely accident. We're glad you're well.

"Our airport limousine was scheduled to meet your flight, but news came that the flight you were on exploded at the gate. Sorry our driver wasn't there to pick you up."

The clerk types a while on the hotel computer and after changing pages and typing more he says, "Our rooms are all filled because of the medical convention tomorrow."

Now I become agitated and say, "The room is prepaid with guaranteed late arrival. I expect you to find something for me tonight."

The clerk goes to the back room and another man comes out to greet me.

"We have a room for you, sir. I really must apologize for the mix-up. You can have the only room that isn't booked.

"That would be no extra charge for the Presidential Penthouse Suite.

"I am the Hotel Manager, Mr. Mims. Ask for me if there is anything more we can do."

Upon checking into the room, I notice the view from the floor to ceiling windows is spectacular and I waste no time slipping into the plush white complimentary robe and closing the curtains.

I turn on the 52 inch 3D television and start watching the news.

The Anchor Reporter is telling of the tragedy occurring at the airport this morning. It's about the flight I was scheduled to fly on.

The reported says, "An airline investigation is in progress today involving an explosion at the gate when an airliner attempted to depart. The freak accident is being investigated by the Air Traffic Safety Administration. The cause of the explosion according to the Safety Board findings is determined to be a defective landing gear release latch?"

The reporter looks off stage quizzically and gestures for a confirmation. Another reporter picks up the story and continues the delivery, "That's right, Chet. The report states that the explosion was caused by a faulty landing gear release latch. It was determined that there was no foul play involving the incident." Off camera there is an exchange unseen by the television audience.

The Anchor Reporter mutters something about flying saucers being weather balloons and other obvious cover ups insulting our intelligence.

His boss in the control room sternly warns him over his ear-bud earpiece to just read and report the news exactly as it's written. The boss warns him, "You are a reporter, not a damned commentator!"

There is a tap at the door and I ask, "Who is it?"

A voice says, "A complimentary bottle of wine from the Hotel Manager, sir."

I look through the peephole and see a uniformed bellhop standing with a bottle of wine. Feeling a bit paranoid, I open the door and thank him.

It looks like a bottle of their finest wine and as I decant it, I can smell the bouquet of a very special and properly stored bottle of vintage wine.

I feel pampered in my plush robe, drinking my vintage wine and watching my big screen 3D TV.

I awaken early and refreshed.

My taxi greets me at the Valet stand.

I arrive at the conference center promptly at 7:00 AM with my presentation in hand.

The first person I see is my old college friend and Fraternity Brother, Kevin Farmer. Kevin has done well for himself and now owns the largest corporate complex for making and supplying medical equipment, Farmer Industries.

Kevin greets me with surprise and says, "My God! You arrived safely. Did you enjoy your trip?

"We had to cancel your slot when we were notified of your premature demise yesterday."

I stagger backward and stand in shock for a moment. "Why am I the only person who thinks I should still be alive right now?

"News of my death is traveling faster than I am.

"Who says I am dead? When did they call?"

Kevin stops me in the midst of my panic to answer, "The head of the conference committee called us. We were told yesterday morning. It comes as quite a shock.

"We are putting together a little eulogy to deliver when it's your time to speak."

My face goes white and I stutter a bit.

Then I speak in a whisper, "My flight was an afternoon flight. You were notified of my death even before I left for the airport."

Kevin gives me a look of deep concern and motions for me to sit down.

Kevin says quietly, almost in a whisper, "Tell me everything."

I recount the entire trip along with all the near misses and the strange encounter in the Limo with the man who assured him he would not live to present at the conference and left with a grin.

Kevin thinks for a minute and exclaims, "We have to get you out of here! I suggest you stay at my place in the valley while I try to find out who your friends are."

I say, "For a while I thought I might just be paranoid. Which friends are you referring to?"

Kevin gives me a warm smile and says, "Your machine can change the face of the world as we know it. No more suffering, no more disease, no more untimely death.

"But for the Government it means staggering increases in the payout of social security, unemployment, disability, welfare and more. The pharmaceutical industry will go bankrupt overnight along with the hospital industry and the medical industry across the board will be transformed from a treatment driven business to a simple referral business for the cure.

"Your machine will destroy the economy of the rich while it offers financial relief to the majority of the poor."

I start to get up from my seat saying, "It would damned well destroy your business, wouldn't it?"

Kevin puts his hand on my shoulder and says, "Gill, if we can pull it off and get your machine to market. We would be the richest two people in the country.

"We can get sole manufacturing rights to your invention and license it out to everyone else.

"All we need to do is copy the licensing practices used by the developers of computer operating systems.

"We don't have to manufacture anything ourselves, just take in the royalties and license fees and go after anyone who tries to steal our business.

"We can not only cash in on the sale of every machine made, but we can take a royalty fee for every treatment that results in a cure.

"The makers of software compilers charge a royalty for every piece of software created for commercial distribution using their product. The compiler developers argue that without their product, the software doesn't work.

"We can do the same with a per-use license fee. I can put my legal team together on this project and we can pave the way to the future for both you and Farmer Industries."

Kevin offers his handshake saying, "Gill, apparently I'm not your best friend. I'm your only friend right now."

I take his hand, give him a nod and smile. My old Fraternity Brother comes to my rescue. Who knew?

"Just sit right here while I make the arrangements for you to be provided with transportation to my place in the valley. You'll be safe there until I can make arrangements to secure your safety.

"Everyone seems to be trying to kill you right now, but once we secure the legal means to manufacture the machine, there won't be any advantage to eliminating you." Kevin says as he picks up the conference room phone.

He dials a number and says, "Nancy, have Andy bring the car around and take my friend here to my place in the valley. I want you to stay with him and provide any administrative assistance he might need.

"Don't let anyone see you leaving and don't let anyone follow you. Make sure Gill has anything he wants to be comfortable. Before you leave call Iron Wall Security and tell them to guard Mr. Bennett with their lives."

Two gigantic men walk into the conference room and stand by the exit. They seem unusually tall and broad at the shoulders and both men smile warmly. I see the butt of a gun for a moment inside the jacket that one of the men is wearing.

Kevin looks over at the men and says, "Take him out the alley exit and keep him safe.

"Make sure no one sees you leaving.

"Keep him safe. He's a very important man."

The car arrives and one of the men opens the door with a big grin and motions for Nancy and me to enter.

I settle into the rich leather seat in the back of the stretched Limousine.

The windows are so dark you can't see in, but you can see out just fine. There are cigars, a TV and a small wet bar.

The two gigantic men are smiling again. When I reach over to open the window, the window doesn't open.

One of the men says, "Sorry for the inconvenience, sir. We can provide you with a cool breeze if you like. The windows are over an inch thick, so they don't open."

With that he touched a switch and a cool refreshing breeze welled up inside the passenger cabin.

He is smiling again and points to the mini-bar. "Go ahead, sir. Mix yourself a drink and relax.

"It's going to be a while before we get there."

All this damned grinning is getting a little spooky. Maybe they are trying to maintain a pleasant atmosphere and put me at ease, but it's having just the opposite effect.

Nancy is quietly drinking a glass of wine and looking out the window at the scenery as we glide down the street of the rural community. She is remarkably beautiful with locks of blond hair that tend to momentarily cover one eye from time to time. It's an incredibly alluring vision. The bright blue eyes are large and deep. Her skin is fair and she is dressed in a conservatively cut gray business suit with tasteful white pumps.

It seems unusual for a lady with this level of sophistication to be devoid of jewelry of any kind.

There is something very compelling about her blend of conservatism and raw sexual attraction.

Chapter 2 My Life in Hiding

I enjoy a scotch on the rocks and settle back into my seat. In some undetermined amount of time, the Limo turns into an estate of palatial magnitude.

I realize that I have been daydreaming for the entire trip, but seem to feel surprisingly refreshed.

It's hard to determine where the public roads end and the estate roads begin.

There is a security gate and the car proceeds inside until it comes to a huge mansion.

The circular driveway and surrounding grounds are perfectly manicured and there is an assortment of strange large lawn ornaments peppered here and there.

My eyes adjust and I realize that the ornaments are various armored vehicles. There is an unoccupied helipad in the center of the circular driveway.

A man is dressed in black with an emblem on his jacket reading, "Iron Wall Security." He smiles and says, "You will be safe here, sir.

"I have to ask you for your cell phone. We can't allow anyone to know of your whereabouts."

He takes the phone and turns it off to prevent the GPS locator in the phone from functioning.

He looks irritated and remarks, "I tell these people to make sure and disable all cell phones before they bring anyone here. Might as well put searchlights on the lawn and runway lights on the driveway! Someone may have tracked your cell phone to this location."

He smiles warmly again and says, "You will be safe here, sir."

It's actually beginning to cause me to feel creepy, the way everyone keeps smiling as though there is some kind of private joke.

Back at the conference Kevin is busy on the phone with his legal team. "Look Al, we need to get this thing locked in as soon as possible. I want a contract by Friday.

"Be at my place in the valley tonight with a draft and let's get the particulars on this machine and how it works.

"When the smoke clears I want to own the rights to manufacture this damned thing.

"Pack a bag because you might be there a while.

"We need to work the best deal we can, either by royalty or by doing a complete buyout. Let's see how cheaply we can get it done. I don't want to give that stupid geek a dime more than I have to" Kevin lamented.

Kevin dials the phone again and barks, "Is he there yet? Keep him there and don't let him talk to anyone. Don't let him go anywhere and keep him occupied any way you can. Drug him if you have to, but keep him under wraps."

Once again Kevin dials and speaks to his Documentation Group Manager and Engineering Team Leader, "Bill, I need you to be at my place in the valley with four of your best draftsmen and Tech-Manual Writers.

"Have Ed bring your hottest two designers along with you. We're going to document the strangest machine you ever saw and draft a set of plans.

"If we use our 3D Chipset we have a chance to expand the functionality.

"I want you each to pack a bag because you might be there a while."

Kevin makes one last call to the company Doctor and says, "Phil, I need you at my place in the valley tonight for a special meeting.

"Bring a full set of medications with you, just in case we need them and pack a bag."

Kevin hangs up the phone and smiles.

He walks to the conference center auditorium where his design teams are presenting the new 3D Chipset to the scientific community for the first time.

Among the presentation team is a man who is slightly taller and slightly better proportioned than the others. His name is Ralph.

He steps up to the microphone and scans the room with his eyes and smiles.

He speaks with a voice that is deep and resonant.

He says, "My name is Ralph and I am a synthetic human. I am made possible by the 3D Chipset we are featuring here today.

"At the conclusion of today's presentation I will answer any questions you might have concerning the technology, that is, any question pertaining to our technology that isn't proprietary."

The audience is enthralled because Ralph was one of the more popular people in the room when they were all having refreshments and socializing before the conference began. No one guessed for a moment he wasn't human.

Ralph draws a breath and continues, "Solid state integration is accomplished by laying circuits on a thin layer of silicon Then connecting wires are attached to the pins for connection to the outside of the chip.

"Devices are made by putting chips on a backboard in clusters and each performs their special function. This takes up a lot of space creates a lot of heat."

Ralph continues on, "We have developed a super dense and much faster switching technology creating no heat and utilizing only electrostatic switching circuits that we build at the atomic level using nanotechnology.

"The magic is accomplished by laying circuits on a thin layer of silicon and then connecting wires to pins for connection to the outside of the chip, but that's where the similarity ends."

"We lay circuits in layers over the chip at the base forming a combination of vertical and horizontal circuits upward to form a cubic design that can be thousands of layers thick and looks like a tiny black block.

"Because the connections and junctions are only a couple of atoms thick, there is almost no heat generated in any on the junctions during the avalanche effect. We call it 3D Chipset technology."

The crowd stands and applauds loudly for a couple of minutes. Ralph walks from the stage and sits in the front row of the auditorium.

Another man steps up and speaks, "In case anyone is curious, using the 3D Chipset, we have condensed the space required to make Ralph's brain into a slightly smaller area than the rest of us require for our brains."

The man pauses for effect and then continues, "Ralph has an I.Q. of 168 and we could have made him smarter, but we wanted to keep the weight of his brain down to match that of our own so he could look and move the way the rest of us do.

"It represents a whole new technology that no one has ever imagined or attempted before."

Kevin makes his way to the roof of the convention center where his helicopter waits and climbs aboard. The rotors spin to life and they lift off in the direction of the nearby valley wholly owned by Farmer Industries.

At the mansion in the valley, Nancy and I are sitting out by the pool enjoying small talk. I am amazed to hear that she is well versed in physics and engineering.

My impression is that this intelligent person is being used in an Administrative Assistant position when she is apparently qualified to head a project.

Out of the sky a dot appears, grows to become a Farmer Industries helicopter and settles gently on the helipad in front of the mansion.

Kevin has returned to his place in the valley in time to enjoy dinner with me.

After dinner we retire to the living room where Kevin asks me how I feel about forming a partnership with him.

Kevin says, "My wealth is built on the understanding that I keep the richest of the technologies close to the vest. I don't let the secret of their success out to anyone.

"People have to come to me as their only source for 3D Chipsets because they need the chipsets to make the products they sell.

"Your machine is an exception to that rule.

"It isn't what it is that makes it worthwhile, but what it does. People don't buy the machine; they buy the results the machine provides."

I say, "It's the old saying; we sell the sizzle, not the steak, right?"

Kevin responds, "That's exactly right."

Kevin goes on saying, "We need to make a few prototypes and then sell the machines outright and also the rights to manufacture them to other companies on a royalty basis. Gill, I want the exclusive right to sell licenses to manufacture this machine. We will share in the profits from the sale of these licenses. I also want you and me to share the exclusive right to earn royalties for the use of this machine. What do you say?"

I am taken by surprise by the offer and begin to feel angry.

"Before you speak, let me share a couple of things with you.

"Your life is in danger. Everyone is out to kill you right now because you are a threat to their existence.

"Your machine can't help anyone sitting at the university. The university won't allow you to convert it to a treatment center any more than you already have."

I nod and say, "That's a good point."

Kevin says, "They tolerated you because it was experimental. You can't even sell the damned machine because you can't manufacture them.

"Even if you decide to make them and productize them, you have better things to do than run a factory.

"Let me repeat this one more time. Your life is in danger. What other options do you have?"

I ask, "Why do you want to sell the rights to manufacture this machine to our competitors?"

He smiles and says, "Gill, remember? We aren't selling the steak, we're selling the sizzle. We can't make these machines fast enough to meet the demand.

"The profits from sales aren't the thing that will make us rich, it's the royalty that we are paid every time the machine is used to save a life.

"I want as many machines out there as possible so when they are used to save human lives in addition to animals they will be available to the clinics across the country."

I begin to understand we are planning for the future and positioning ourselves to save the lives of millions of suffering people.

Nancy and I are going over some of the aspects of the design used in the Cure. She seems to have an immediate grasp of the concept along with the best possible implementations. She tells me, "This machine is a blessed miracle. We have to get this out to the people of the world. Just imagine the suffering it will eliminate."

Her comment sums up my feelings from the very beginning. Whatever it takes to get this product to market will be justified.

She gets a bit of a faraway look and says, "Farmer Industries has a special component that can make the machine better than it already is.

"I can't tell you about it just yet because it's a trade secret, but just you wait."

I hear Kevin call me into a conference room where he says, "I want you to meet Al. Al is my Attorney and he is here to make sure we get this all down in writing, signed and agreed to."

Al puts his briefcase on the table and says, "The question isn't should you sell out to Kevin. The question is just how much will it take?

"Kevin's sales and royalties come at a cost. Kevin has to bear up under the financial burden of doing business."

Kevin injects, "It costs a lot of money to run a factory and build a sales team with the cost of labor, commissions and all the rest."

Al looks over his glasses at me.

I've seen that body language before. Al is looking to see if I'm buying his line of B.S. I say, "It's pretty obvious who you're here to represent. I think I need a Lawyer to represent me here."

Al sits back in his seat and says, "Sure, Gill. We can wait for your Lawyer to get here before we all begin. Who do you trust right now? Let's give him a call and get him over here."

Kevin shifts uneasily in his seat. The last thing he wants is anyone from the outside messing things up right now.

"Kevin says, "Gill, Gill, Gill. You're alive right now because no one knows you're here. I'm not trying to steal your design.

"I'm trying to give you back your life and share in a mutually beneficial business arrangement. I think you're smart enough to decide what's fair. What do you say?"

I think a moment and say, "Let's see what you come up with and we can go from there. If it looks fair then I'll sign the contract."

Kevin responds with, "The only way we can go forward here is for me to determine what my costs are and what my margins are.

"If I'm going to make an offer, we need to get the entire manufacturing process down on paper. To do that you need to work with my documentation and design teams."

I agree this is reasonable and the work commences on the documentation and design details.

Kevin tells me, "The manufacturing elements are being determined by triangulating the parts, processes and finance department numbers. We should have the information we need in a matter of hours."

Later in the day Kevin and Al came and sat down again with me to strike a deal.

After laying it all out and determining the margins, the contract proposal suggested a forty percent yield on the gross profits for me.

I just want to end this fear for my life and want to return to my lab and continue my work.

I say, "Sure Kevin, make sure I retain ownership and you can have an exclusive right, but only as long as you live and are able to run Farmer Industries.

Your contract has to allow for audits by my finance team and in the event of your death or lack of capacity to perform, I have to acquire all rights."

Kevin looks upset and lashes out with, "I saved your neck when everyone was trying to kill you and now you suggest that I might not be honest with you when it's time to pay you? What the hell are you thinking?"

My face gets hot and I'm feeling embarrassed, so I say, "For crying out loud. I am grateful for your help, but you're a business man.

"You know what it takes to make a profit and what it takes to keep a relationship healthy. If you want to do business with me then let me have some sense of security."

Kevin throws up his hands and says, "Fine, just sign it."

That night Kevin was on the 6:00 PM Evening News being interviewed. He says, "Doctor Professor Gill Bennett is alive and well.

"Farmer Industries has acquired the exclusive manufacturing and sales agreement for 'The Cure'.

"Professor Bennett will be returning to his teaching job with the University and will have no further direct involvement with sales and marketing of the Cure."

As I'm leaving the mansion to return to my home, I am given a check for $500,000 as a down payment on the contract with Farmer Industries.

I am driven home in the company Limo with the driver smiling broadly and talking a string of small talk that went on for the entire trip.

It's great to be home in familiar surroundings. Things have been getting a lot more exciting than I like so I decide to make myself a drink and stay home to relax and unwind.

As I'm watching the news and sipping my drink the story comes on about my reappearance on the scene with an exclusive Farmer Industries contract.

There is a knock at the door. I'm inclined to ignore it, but the sound of the TV is giving my presence away.

I go to the peek hole and look through to see a tall lean man with ruddy skin and bright blazing blue eyes.

I ask, "Who is it?"

I hear him say, "Lieutenant Daggett. Professor Bennett, I presume. May I have a word with you?"

He's wearing a trench coat, a stern expression and holding up a small black leather folder with a gold badge next to an ID card with his picture on it.

"I wasn't planning on having company Officer Daggett. Can you come back tomorrow? I've had a hard day" I plead.

"It would appear that you've had quite a few hard days recently. This won't take long Professor. I have a few questions that really can't wait."

I surrender in despair and open the door.

The Lieutenant Daggett studies me as he comes through the door and produces a small pocket notepad and pen.

Something about his eyes makes me uneasy. It's as though they can see right through me.

In a bid to be sociable, I offer, "Would you care for a drink, a coffee or anything else Officer?"

He levels his stare and ignores my question.

When he speaks it comes across harshly, "I have a few questions about your recent activities.

"You reported to Airport Security that your life was in danger. Then you were reported dead, but we couldn't find any evidence of your funeral. The report said that you died in an Airport explosion, but Airport Security tells me you were not on that airplane."

I interrupt him saying, "Yes, I am alive. So you come here with some bizarre recounting of my experience. What is your point?"

You also never made your appearance at the conference where your eulogy was read when it was your time to speak. You should have been there Professor; I was told there wasn't a dry eye in the house."

I fidget in my seat and he continues; "Now you're back as though nothing happened.

"We don't like following up on false reports. You've made a lot of false reports lately, Professor. What's up?"

My uneasiness intensifies and I shift again in my seat. I say, "Yes, I'm alive, but I'm not the one who reported my death! You can't pin that on me."

The Lieutenant shouts, "You're up to something and I am going to find out what it is."

With that I say, "Thank you for stopping by. Come again soon," and I open the door.

The Lieutenant says, "You can order me to leave and I have to go because there is no warrant, yet. I have a feeling I'll be back soon."

The Lieutenant leaves and I am finally alone again at last, but not as relaxed as before.

In the morning I stop off at the bank to deposit the check.

When I arrive back at the University, the Dean greets me with the news that there has been a terrible accident in the lab.

We enter the lab and have to step over the debris still lying on the floor.

Workers are cleaning up the tangled mess which consists mainly of my machine.

I am horror stricken demanding to know, "What the hell happened to my machine and where are the drawings and reports I had in the filing cabinet here?"

The Dean appears distressed and answers, "It happened last night. We figure it was about 10:00 PM."

I stop and think a moment and remark, "So that is only four hours after the evening news broadcast. It sure isn't taking them long to get back to the task of destroying the concept of instant healing. They just want to make sure I don't try to get it approved for use on humans."

The Dean told me to take the rest of the week off to get things settled back home. "The cost of the MRI machine alone is more than we can afford to replace" the Dean says.

I clean up my office which has been turned inside out. Anything pertaining to the machine is missing.

At the end of the day I leave to go home.

As I go to my car I stop in my tracks. The driver's door is open and there is no one around. I pull out my cell phone and dial 911 and wait. I don't want to have another car explode and possibly hurt someone or any of the cars around it.

The Police arrive and I tell them about the time the car exploded outside the pet shop. The two Police Officers go to the car and look it over without disturbing it. These seem to be the same two Officers that responded to the last incident.

The Bomb Squad arrives and tape off the area while they work on the car.

The two Police Officers come over to me and ask, "What are you talking about when you say this happened before?"

I recounted, "My car exploded a couple of weeks ago outside of a pet shop."

The cops stop me and say, "There is no report on file regarding your car exploding, we checked on the incident you're claiming. Don't go involving the Police in your paranoid fantasies. Your car was broken into. It happens every day." They smile and leave the scene.

When I look over the car, I find some papers missing that pertain to the machine. A couple of old customer contracts allowing me to treat their dogs are also missing.

I drive home in despair. It looks more and more like Kevin is right. Kevin seems to be my only friend right now.

I call my Principal Engineer over at the university and ask, "How is Rags doing? I'm not going to be able to treat him right now."

My Engineer says, "Rags died two days ago. He was pretty bad off. The owner hasn't called to see how the dog is doing either.

"We took him to a vet to see if there is anything we could do, but he was too far gone."

I hang up and wipe away a tear. Having never gotten to treat Rags doesn't mean I killed him. It just means I never got to save him. I feel terrible.

As I pull into my driveway I notice a light on upstairs in the bedroom. I pull out my cell phone and dial 911 again.

Once again the Police come and it's the same two Officers that responded back at the University.

I say, "Sorry to call you again so soon, but it looks like someone or some group of people are breaking into everything I own."

The older of the two Officers says, "What the hell are you talking about? We've never received a call from you today."

I ask if they can accompany me through the house and make sure it's safe to enter.

The two cops go in with me and find the place turned inside out. The younger of the two cops says, "Wow! Someone was looking for something, that's for sure". The older of the two Officers nudges his partner and shakes his head, "NO."

I am fit to be tied. Every time I call the Police these two smiling Officers show up and do nothing.

"How can they not remember the call from earlier today?

I'm feeling defeated and say, "Alright. Thanks for coming out. Will there be a report on this incident?"

The older Officer's face lights up and he smiles broadly as he says, "Of course there will. We have to file a report on every call. You may be hearing from one of our Detectives regarding this break in."

The younger of the two Officers smiles and says, "Sorry for your loss, sir."

I'm beginning to become suspicious of all the people grinning at me at all the strangest times.

I open up my cell phone and realize that the SIMM chip is not the same one I had in here before.

I plug in the cell phone's SIMM chip to the module programmer in the computer and discover a subtle change in the programming.

When I dial 911, I am actually dialing a number in the nearby valley instead.

"Something nasty is going on here" I say to myself.

My phone has never been out of my sight until they took it and held it for me at the mansion.

They had to make the switch before my trip to the valley because strange things were happening when the car bomb exploded. The SIMM chip was swapped, but when and by whom?

If the Police I've been calling are not the real Police and they are coming from the valley, then they have to be Kevin's people.

If the incident they are responding to is part of a cover up, then Kevin is responsible for the car bomb and all the times there was a break in.

It dawns on me that all of the attempts on my life and the break in at the University are Kevin's doing. Kevin set this whole thing up.

I realize that I am stuck in a contract with someone who is trying to kill me. I'm also thinking that until I get some proof, I won't be able to get out of the agreement or have Kevin arrested for attempted murder.

Then I stagger back on my feet and almost fall.

It was Kevin that was responsible for the airliner at the gate exploded killing everyone aboard along with anyone within range of the blast.

It was Kevin that was responsible for the disappearance of the Veterinarian and his staff, and everyone else who disappeared without a trace.

It was Kevin that was responsible for the total destruction of the University lab and the theft of everything pertaining to the machine I created.

I have to sit down to let it all sink in.

"This man is the Devil himself. He's a mass murderer. If I tip my hand he will kill me on the spot" I mutter under my breath.

The only way to get out of this mess is to play along for now. I need to get inside of Kevin's factory and figure out what's going on and what I can do about it.

The next morning Kevin invites me to Farmer Industries to check out the new machine he has created from the plans drawn up at the valley mansion.

I am greeted by Kevin as he enters the lobby and I am escorted to the lab where an exact duplicate of my original machine sits.

I say, "Is it a working prototype?"

Kevin says, "It's a perfect specimen. We ran a couple of sick animals through it and they are fine now. Would you like to meet my principal Engineer and Team Leader?"

He leaves the lab and returns with an engineer dressed in a white smock.

I walk over and shake the engineer's hand.

Kevin says, "Gill, meet Bob. Bob has been able to duplicate your machine and treatments based on the information you provided."

Bob looks over at me and says, "Would you like to take a tour of the lab and manufacturing facility?"

I nod enthusiastically and follow him through the double doors at the end of the room.

We enter a large lab with equipment all around the room. In the center are rows of computers in racks that go almost to the ceiling. Cable racks take up space along the top of the computers and seem to run everywhere. They are filled with various colored cables.

The room is filled with the sound of rushing air from the ventilation system used to cool the wealth of hardware.

Bob leads me over to the wall where there is a huge machine.

Bob explains, "This is the 3D Sputtering machine. We put a silicon wafer in the machine and the scanner etches the wafer and then starts to lay down layer after layer of materials from insulators to semiconductor material and chromium.

"We can create cubes of semiconductor so dense they replace millions of semiconductor chips.

"Without the wiring between the old chip design methods we have speeds that surpass the human brain in their ability to complete complex functions.

"The 3D Chipsets are so complex, in fact, that they have to run overnight on the tester to verify that all the functions work correctly."

I am impressed and notice that the lab workers are all smiling.

Then there is an accident in the lab and sparks are followed by a curl of smoke.

The technician's eyes light up and she grins enthusiastically.

I look over at Bob and say, "What the hell is that? Everyone is so damned happy when things go wrong around here."

Bob laughs and says, "Kevin has very few human workers.

"You never noticed that these people are all androids because they are so perfect.

"Our public speaker is also an android. His name is Ralph. The only comment we've heard regarding Ralph is his annoying tendency to smile at inappropriate times. We're working on that problem."

I say, "Yes, I can see why having the strangest people smiling at the strangest times might give them away."

Bob laughs and nods. "They frankly get on my nerves at times. It's spooky."

Before I can think better of asking, I ask, "Are they capable of killing anyone?"

Bob stops smiling and looks quizzically at me, "Exactly why are you asking me that?"

I immediately regret my mistake and think fast to overcome it.

I start to backpedal and attempt to lighten the mood with, "Just curious I guess. I wondered if they could be used as soldiers in the military."

Bob visibly relaxes and says, "We have an active contract with the government.

"Why would anyone use an android to commit a crime of passion?"

I decide that his question is rhetorical and not to answer, but I'm thinking that many violent crimes are crimes of indifference, not hate.

We move on to the manufacturing area and I can't help but notice there are dozens of chambers for administering the cure.

I ask, "Where are all the MRI and MRE machines to go with these chambers?"

"The MRI and MRE machines are integrated into the chambers. We used 3D Chips to replace both machines.

"We also automated the job of programming the proper frequencies to eliminate malignancies and harmful bacteria.

"The 100 Exabyte memory layers have more room than we need to store every possible invader a body could endure."

I say, "That's an impressive upgrade. I always had to work out the key frequencies one by one."

Don't feel bad, Gill. We did a bang up job because we have a full staff of engineers to work on it. You did what you did alone. I'm very impressed with how much progress you achieved in the short time you had."

I return home and wonder how I am ever going to turn this mess around.

The first thing I have to do is nibble away at this wall of fantasy that Kevin has created.

I decide to go in to work the next day.

Upon arriving at the university, I go out back to the university dumpster and throw in a burning match.

At the first sign of a curl of smoke, I call 911 from my cell phone and then go inside to my office where I also pick up the phone and dial 911. "The best I can hope is that the timing is right", I say to myself.

The Dean comes by and asks, "Why did you come to work today? I say to take the next two days off."

I conjure up my best blank face and say, "I had to get something from my desk. I'll be out of here as soon as possible. Forget I was ever here."

The Dean leaves my office mumbling.

I leave the door unlocked and head out back to the dumpster.

If the real Police check out my story they have to see that it was possible for the phony Police to have made the call from my office.

Within minutes I am greeted by the same two Officers as were responding to my former 911 calls.

The older of the two Officers confronts me and asks, "Why did you call 911."

I point to the dumpster ablaze within their full view.

The Older Police Officer says, "We already called for the Fire Department."

Next the phony Fire Department arrives on the scene and proceeds to put the fire out.

Now I see why the smiling synthetic humans give me the creeps. There is something almost cartoon like about the smiling faces as they battle the blaze, almost reminiscent of the seven dwarfs on their way to the diamond mine in the movie, "Snow White and the Seven Dwarfs."

Until Farmer Industries figures out how to stop the grinning epidemic among their androids, they might as well write android on their foreheads.

The real Police show up along with the Fire Department and ask, "Who called 911?"

I figure, what the hell, I decide to have a little fun. I say, "Those two Officers over there asked to use my phone and the older one called it in."

The Police Lieutenant looked over at the two phony Officers and says, "Who the hell are they?"

The Sergeant shouts, "Hey! You two! Up against the car and spread your feet!"

The Lieutenant is on his phone calling for backup when the two imposters smile widely and draw their guns.

The Sergeant pulls his service weapon and opens fire on the two imposters who are firing back.

I hit the ground and remained still. I think I lit the fuse on a bad situation.

More Police cars come swiftly with their lights and sirens blasting.

Within seconds there are about eight Police returning fire at the two phony cops who are standing their ground.

Now the phony Fire Department gets involved and starts spraying the real Police with fire hoses.

A couple of the real cops are caught in the force of the spray and are being driven across the ground, spinning as they go.

Then the eight phony Firemen attack the real Police with axes and shovels.

More Police cars are coming on the scene and it's a free for all.

It's becoming apparent that the phony cops can't shoot straight because none of the real cops are hit.

Then the two phony cops begin to twitch and vibrate, emitting smoke and sparks as they gyrate in a manner that could be a new dance craze. The two phony cops fall to the ground.

It looks like the water from the hoses didn't help when the phony cops open wounds began to fill with the liquid. They lay on the ground grinning like broken dolls.

Pretty soon there are two phony Police Officers and eight phony Firemen on the ground. It's obvious the ten bodies are not human.

The Police Chief is on the scene by now and has his hand on his head in a gesture of utter confusion.

The Chief shouts, "Who the hell do we call now? We can't call the Coroner or an ambulance or a hearse.

"Have these damned things transported to Headquarters for examination.

"I want to know what they are and where they came from."

I returned home and poured myself a nice strong drink. I eased back in my easy chair and turned on the TV.

I wait for the evening news. I want to hear how they report this one.

My phone rings and its Kevin. He sounds angry and asks, "What the hell did you do this morning over at the university?"

I say, "What do you mean?

"I'm a little busy right now. What happened?"

He falls silent for a minute and says, "Never mind. I'll have to get back to you. Perhaps I was mistaken."

Chapter 3 Free At Last

I am relaxing and getting a little drowsy from the drink I made. The 6:00 News is coming on and I want to see what they report from this morning. I turn on the TV and the evening news comes with footage from the eye in the sky.

The reporter is shouting into the microphone about a shootout and a riot at the university between Police and Fire Department personnel.

You can see the footage with all the uniformed Officers firing at each other and at the Firemen on the ground.

One of the Officers begins to vibrate and as they zoom in on him, he begins to do what looks like the funky chicken with sparks shooting from him, and then he falls to the ground.

The next shot is of Kevin being hauled away in handcuffs.

I smile and say to myself, "Guess they found out where the androids are coming from."

The news commentator says, "No one was injured in the shootout and both the Police Chief and the Fire Chief are both declining to comment saying, "This matter is still under investigation."

The next day my phone is ringing again and it's Kevin. He sounds angry and asks, "What were you doing at the university yesterday? I know you had something to do with that whole fiasco."

I just say, "Yea, What was that, Kevin. This is the second time you called and asked me about it. Are you involved in that crazy stunt?"

Kevin seems a bit heated. It's time to do something before the entire situation gets out of control. It looks like it's time to give Kevin something else to think about for a while.

I go shopping and buy four cheap pay-as-you-go cell phones. Next I buy four cheap digital recorders. Each phone and each recorder are purchased at separate stores located at separate locations with cash to minimize the chance that the items can be traced back to me.

I take all of the items to my little hobby lab in the basement and go to work. I still have the number my phone calls when I dial 911. I program the number into four of the cheap cell phones and record a voice distress message off the computer using the "read out loud" program. The voice can't be traced to anyone. I use four cheap timers to activate the cheap disposable cell phones.

At 2:38 PM the cheap timers will trigger the phones to place a call to the phony 911 number and summon Kevin's phony Police along with his phony Fire Department using the recorded distress messages.

After four minutes, at 2:42 PM, the phone will hang up and trigger the phone again which will dial 911 for the real Police and play the prerecorded messages again.

I fill each of these four boxes with phosphorous and ignition material set to explode in flames at exactly 2:46 PM. The fire will burn in excess of 2000 degrees inside the dumpster at each of the four target locations. At this extreme temperature there won't be enough of the firing device for them to examine.

These four locations are in the perimeter of the city, but with easy access to the main expressway out of the valley that skirts the city. The boxes will burn so hot that no trace of the phones or other electronics inside the boxes will be usable as evidence.

The ignition of the boxes will start the dumpster and all of its contents burning immediately with flames six feet high. The column of smoke erupting from the dumpster will be seen for miles.

This will bring Kevin's phony Police along with his phony Fire Department to the scene ahead of the real Police and Fire Department.

This should ensure that the phony Police are already on the scene when the real Police arrive, resulting in four separate circus fiascos identical to the one that had him arrested the first time.

If I can't prove Kevin is the mastermind behind the mass murders, then I have to let Kevin put on a show for the authorities and demonstrate to them how he actually perpetrates his techno-crimes.

I will not plant evidence to get him wrongly convicted; I will merely create the opportunity, much like the Police use "Bait Cars." In a surreptitious fashion I will merely set the stage, light the spotlight, and allow Kevin's (Farmer Industry's) automatons to act out their evil deeds.

I would think that ought to do it. I need to have Kevin where he can't try to kill me anymore.

I begin to smile and say to myself, "There, that should do it."

I rent a car to reduce the likelihood that the tire prints will be matched up. I dress in women's clothing in case I'm seen. I wear shoes two sizes too big for me in case I leave footprints. I wear thirty five pounds of lead around my waist to make my weight appear heavier in the mud.

At around 9:20 AM, wearing rubber gloves, I throw each of these boxes I made, set to go off at exactly 2:46 PM into the dumpster at the target locations. The four target locations are in the perimeter of the city, but with easy access to the main road out of the valley. The dumpsters are well behind locked gates and not scheduled for pickup until Friday morning.

Today being Saturday and the four businesses in question being closed today, the likelihood of anyone being injured are nonexistent.

I go home and change back into my regular clothing, return the rental car and drive back to the house. It's 10:14 PM.

Things are pretty busy out at Farmer Industries and the factory along with Kevin's office is having a regular workday today.

I call Kevin and ask him if I can come out to the factory and use their lab.

Kevin says, "Sure you can. I've been working on a lab you can use. We may need your help with some improvements we want to integrate into our machines.

While I'm working in the Farmer Industries lab, Kevin knows where I am and what I'm busy doing, so there is no reason for him to think I'm involved in the drama that's about to unfold at each of the four locations around the city

Kevin's phony Police rush to answer the phony 911 calls originating from the four dumpster bombs.

Then at each of the four locations the real Police respond and end up confronting the phony Police.

A rerun of the university circus ensues. It's a free for all and the news media helicopters are getting it all on video tape.

I call Kevin in his office at 2:30 PM and suggest we get coffee saying, "It's time for a break and just thought I'd like to chat a while." We head on up to the company cafeteria to get coffee. As I watch Kevin getting his coffee he grabs a piece of pie.

I smile and think, "Enjoy your pie. There might be pie in jail, but there will be no pie in hell."

We talk for a good half hour and then the Police show up in the cafeteria to arrest Kevin again. This time they look pretty serious and Kevin looks totally confused because I've been here all day.

By now Kevin is wondering who is setting him up. I think about how he used his phony Police and his phony people and his phony attempts to make me believe everyone in the world is trying to kill me. I think about how many people he has killed and there is a strange satisfaction knowing that I'm using the tools he created to put him where he belongs, if only for a while.

I'm sure glad I put in the clause saying that in the event of Kevin's death or incapacity, I would acquire all the rights to my invention. It also stipulates that I would take over Farmer Industries at that time. What that means is that if Kevin is in the hospital or in prison, I will take over. Poor Kevin is sentenced to twenty five years in prison for arson and other assorted violent felonies. The use of armed automatons to commit a crime was construed at trial in the same manner as using a firearm himself.

I quickly have the matter concerning control of Farmer Industries brought before a Judge who agrees that I am entitled to take over.

Kevin was scheduled to give a press conference outlining a program to cure a test sample of animals of their diseases. There was to be a demonstration. A license deal is to be offered at a discount over the next two years on a trial membership basis.

I have Nancy gather the information needed to present the discount program.

The TV Station is not far from my office so I make the short ride over there. We have a spot on the news to talk about The Cure and what it can mean for animals across the country.

While I am on the air, I am asked, "What will The Cure mean for me and my family in the event of illness in the future?"

I answer with, "The AMA and the Surgeon General have determined that The Cure is not a viable option for humans. We have tried to get this product accepted for public use and we will continue to try." I am hoping the product will be approved for clinical trials soon.

With the interview ended, I return to my office at the university.

Things at the university are on an even keel for the time being. My lab and my staff are busy with several small projects and I am teaching again on a regular schedule.

Kevin was right, you know. I am not interested in running a factory, but have to figure out how to protect my interests and not have to spend my time running a manufacturing facility.

My legal department at Farmer Industries has been busy working on ways to increase revenues by creating new revenue streams.

I receive a call from the White House and a visit from the Secret Service. The military is requiring us to sign a nondisclosure agreement before we can work a deal for the manufacture of Cure Machines to be used by the Defense Department.

They want two units installed at the White House Clinic where they can treat the President and his immediate family in the event of illness.

The Senate and Congress called with a request to sell two machines to each of them because they are exempt from the Food and Drug Administration rulings. They are paying us a monthly fee in lieu of royalties per use.

I am surprised to hear that our political representatives are classed as rulers. Law makers apparently are therefore immune to the restriction governing the treatment of humans.

The sale, along with service contracts and monthly fees, are classified Top Secret.

We are being given a waiver allowing us to not report our earnings received from the White House to the IRS in the interest of national security, as that would constitute a violation of the nondisclosure.

Orders are pouring in from all the world rulers for machines to export overseas to the seat of their governments.

The CIA is screening the orders and approving or disapproving the sale of each machine to ensure our National Security. They want to make sure certain counties don't have access to the technology.

I get the feeling that being allowed to obtain The Cure would represent a powerful bargaining chip in the area of world political and militaristic negotiations. I understand North Korea is becoming more agreeable in their talks.

Our legal team has determined that it is actually legal to offer Cure Insurance for pets across America and in Canada and Mexico.

Our company is in receipt of a license to become an insurance carrier. We now sell our Cure Insurance for the exclusive rescue of insured animals in the event they become sick.

Over the life of all the animals we insure, it pays statistically more than if we treated their ailments in the traditional manner. It's great for us because it assures we will be paid handsomely for every animal out there whether they ever get sick or not.

Now the finance team is calculating the copays for treatment given for those with no Cure Insurance. It's worked out so that if you check into a Cure center without Cure insurance, you are charged ten times the rate negotiated for the insured pets.

The money is rolling in so fast we can't keep our books updated and our manufacturing capacity isn't growing fast enough to supply all the orders coming in. I swear, the faster the money flows into our coffers, the greedier the company is becoming.

I am holding a staff meeting to try and slow the growth of the company and stop finding ways to glean money from pet owners in need of services.

As for my forty percent split on profits, frankly, I haven't even thought of asking for the sixty percent I should be entitled to since I'm doing all the work. What's the difference? Sixty percent of ten billion dollars doesn't feel so different from forty percent of ten billion dollars. How much can I spend in my lifetime?

As we are seated in the big conference room, my department heads and legal team are gathered to hear my message regarding the future strategy of the company.

Nancy is by my side. She and I have been working late for several nights to put this meeting together.

I begin my presentation with, "I want to thank each of you for the magnificent job you're doing. Our profits are through the roof and it's due entirely to your fine efforts.

I've become aware that The Cure is not being offered to everyone who needs it, but is being managed according to the ability of the people's ability to pay. We need to establish centers where the poor can bring their animals and, based on the proof that they can't pay the full fee, we will not only provide healing, but will waive the royalty fee."

A gasp goes up around the room and the Vice President of Finance, Phil Macklin asks to be recognized.

I give him the floor and sit down. "The cost of providing low cost services for the needy would be astronomical. There is the cost of processing the applications and weeding out the ones who can afford it would take a large staff of people to verify the information and pro-rate the treatment. Then there is the triage team of medical people who will need to determine which animals are most critical and establish the priority for treatment. Even after all of this, we have the cost of the machines which will need to be in every population center, and then we would have to have a staff of people to operate the equipment. Although the training required is minimal, they all have to be trained. We will impact our profits by a large margin. We will go bankrupt."

Another question erupts from the floor, "Have you discussed this with Kevin?"

I take a firm stand and answer, "I am running things now. We're going to stop victimizing the people of America by holding their animal's hostage."

The legal team looks like they are each about to have a stroke.

The Vice President of Legal, Al Akken asks for the floor.

I grant him the time to speak. "Many of these patents are already five years old. Let me remind you that a patent is only good for twenty seven years and after that anyone can manufacture and sell our product. If we don't maximize our profits and grow fast enough to squeeze out any upcoming competition, we could well be put out of business. We need to be creating barriers to entry into our field of business, not creating an open market based on charity and good will."

I can't believe the level of resistance. I fire back with, "For crying out loud, Al! Of all people you have to know that we haven't patented the key components of this machine. We have protected our legal interests through the company secrets provision in the law. Your argument is a ploy to persuade anyone who doesn't understand the provision. I hear each of your concerns. Let's be clear about this. We aren't lining our pockets any more. Our pockets are overflowing. Isn't it time we gave a little back?"

Maybe you all entered into this venture with the intention of becoming wealthy. Well, you've succeeded and so have I.

As for me I entered into this venture thinking that one day there will be no more needless suffering in the world. That day is almost here. All we have to do is convince the greedy people in the world that their loved ones need not die without good reason.

We're going to make The Cure so common as to create a political revolution if that's what it takes to get this service extended to every person on the planet.

You've each had your dream come true, now let me have my dream as well.

From this day forth the greed will end. We will make an honest profit and serve the interests of our patients and customers."

I wait, but the applause never comes.

People around the company hate me. They call me bubble head and shun me. Sometimes power and wealth won't even get you false friends. Anyone who ever said it's lonely at the top must have been there.

My phone rings almost every day with special interest groups threatening me if I continue working to get The Cure approved for humans. I am told it will destroy the economy. I agree that the economy is largely based on healthcare and illness. I actually call healthcare wealth-care. It provides little in the way of assistance because the deductibles are way too high and it drains the life out of almost everyone. They take our money and then when we need a return on our investment, they concoct barriers to our eligibility called pre-existing conditions.

They have medicalized every known milestone on the way through life. Menopause is not a disease. Wrinkles and spotting of the skin are not diseases. We watch commercial after commercial promising to cure what ails us and what ails us is the natural process of living a full life. We need The Cure and instead of health insurance we need to sell Cure Insurance. The economy doesn't serve the common person.

I have created a movement across America, Canada and Mexico to legalize the use of The Cure for humans. The Internet is alive with sites and fund raising to provide legal assistance for anyone suffering from a terminal disease, but the courts are not interested in ruling on matters of legislation.

Ads and banners shout the meaning of THE CURE (The Healthy Earth, Caring Until we Rescue Everyone). It's an emotional political issue and I work to keep it that way. There are those who are violently opposed to our mission and will stop at nothing to safeguard the economy.

Not being a complete fool, I have taken six androids from the lab and had them especially trained in self-defense. Their brains are programmed with one thing in mind, safeguarding my life. I call them my Goons. Anywhere you see my car; you see a large black short-limo following me.

I am on my way home from the University and am confronted by an angry mob. The limo stops behind me and six huge men step out and advance on the mob. The largest of the Goons orders the mob to disband.

The apparent mob leader comes forward and strikes one of the Goons across the head with a large steel pipe. The titanium skull of the Goon is unscathed.

The stricken Goon smiles and nods at the man. The pipe is now bent in the middle.

The mob disperses. We move on.

Back at the university, the Dean is not happy with the six men who seem to accompany me everywhere. He says, "These people are not faculty, they are not staff, and they are not students. What are they doing here?"

I respond with, "My life is in constant danger and they are watching over me."

"Are they armed?" he asks.

I answer, "Yes, of course they're armed."

The Dean becomes visibly angry and asks, "Did you know it's a felony to carry a firearm onto university property? The law was passed in the sixties when the most violent of the university riots happened."

I leave the university property immediately along with my Goons.

On the way out of the building the Dean tells me, "You are here to teach, Professor. If you require assistance from people who are not affiliated with the university then you will not be allowed to teach. Make up your mind how you would like to proceed. Good day."

We exit the university grounds. My car followed by the big black limo with the Goons in tow.

We make our way back to my office at Farmer Industries where I can shut out the world long enough to get my head around what's happening.

I tell the secretary that Nancy and I can't be disturbed under any circumstances.

As usual, I have my two Goons standing by in the outer office.

It's time to decide who I am. Am I a university professor? If I am going to be a professor, I have to turn my back on everything else. This means abandoning the dream of saving the world. Am I a captain of industry and a creator of a new technology that needs to be driven to its conclusion? If I am it means turning my back on everything else. This means turning my back on the university and my desire to mold bright young minds.

I agonize for couple of hours, but not alone. Nancy is here. She is listening and nodding. She offers no advice except to remind me of my noble mission.

The choice is clear. There are a lot of good professors that could come in and replace me. There is no other person on the planet who can work the issues needing to be resolved around The Cure. Even though I am tenured at the university, I will have to turn my back on the secure lifestyle that the university provides.

It's time to take the bull by the horns and get my machine to market.

I arrange to meet with the Dean, but decide not to tip my hand right now. I'm going to hear what the Dean has to say before letting him know that I will need to resign.

Before doing that I meet with the legal team and ask what my rights are as a tenured professor. The news is both good and bad. They have a right to shut me out if I insist on having body guards standing by while I'm on campus. They can't fire me, but if I'm not showing up for classes, they can replace me and argue that I'm not living up to the terms of my tenure. I can quit, but wouldn't be entitled to any consideration because it would be a voluntary termination.

The best thing I can do is say as little as possible and let the Dean drive the conversation. I have nothing to lose by waiting him out. I can see it's going to be more about who blinks first than who drives the hardest bargain.

I show up at the university alone for the meeting. It doesn't make sense to bring anyone with me since the crux of the problem is my habit of bringing my own support staff with me to the university.

I left Nancy back at the office with permission to take the day off and find a place to live closer to work.

She says I also needs to pick up a new wardrobe."

Her cost center is being assigned to my office so I can pay her from my budget.

Meeting with the Dean won't be a pleasant experience.

I am entering the exchange with "dirty hands." That means I am in violation of the law, because I have expected to have armed body guards in the building, and that's illegal to start with.

The Dean has a somber demeanor as he enters the room.

I am thinking this is not going to go well, but sit quietly and wait.

The Dean says, "Gill, you've been a valued part of this institution for longer than I have. Your tenure is a valuable asset to us, but we can't have armed body guards occupying the building. What's more, you have become somewhat of a liability here lately. Our lab was trashed and some very valuable equipment was destroyed."

I nod in agreement, but remain silent.

The Dean taps the table with his pen and looks distressed.

I look at him and break my silence, "So where are we headed here? We seem to be at a crossroads and I'm not sure what you're proposing as a solution." I am keeping myself in a neutral position in the negotiation, leaving all the university's options in the Dean's court. My non-committal attitude forces his hand. I'm sure he was hoping I would resign, but I'm saving that option for last in hopes of a better deal.

The Dean emits a small cough, resulting from the tension he is under at the moment. He is looking down at his note pad and speaks, "The Board has advised me that the best we can do is extend you a buyout offer. I would suggest you consider seeking work elsewhere. I have been authorized to sweeten the pie with a two year extended salary offer, plus a $50,000 severance check.

I smile warmly and say, "I love it here, sir. I can understand the difficulty of your situation. I really wish we could come up with some way to keep the relationship alive. Unfortunately I think I'm going to accept your offer as a compromise."

The Dean Opens his briefcase and hands me the termination agreement to sign along with the Cobra forms and other contractual necessities. I feign disappointment and sign the forms.

I enter my office suite back at Farmer Industries and advise my secretary that I'm not to be disturbed.

I have a message from the President of Iron Wall Security marked urgent. I immediately give him a call.

He says, "Gill, I have word that Kevin has been talking to some of the people there at Farmer's. I think something may be brewing."

I say, "Thanks Frank." I put Frank on hold for a moment.

This time I decide to have four Goons in the outer office and two more stationed with my secretary.

Back on the phone with Frank, I tell him, "Things seem to be heating up. The meeting I had with senior management has prompted calls to Kevin at the prison. Kevin is livid with rage about my decision to cut back on some of the potential profits around the Cure marketing strategy. I want the names of the people Kevin has been talking to. I want the phone extension numbers and voice recordings of the conversations from the Farmer Industry's phone tracking system. Also get printed copies of all Email activity, both incoming and outgoing, from each of their computers in the server data base. When you get that information, I want a full background check run on these people and their complete company personnel file on my desk. Do the same with Kevin Farmer. I want a full report in my office by tomorrow morning."

Frank says, "Yes sir. I'll put my best people on it and have it done for you."

It's turning out to be a long day. The stress of all this peril is beginning to get to me. I smile for a moment knowing I was wrong, I'm not paranoid. They are actually out to get me.

My intercom buzzes and the secretary tells me there is a man from Iron Wall Security here to sweep my office for bugs.

I ask her to have him wait a minute because I'm on an important call.

I dial Frank over at Iron Wall Security and ask, "Did you send a man over here to sweep my office for bugs?"

Frank says, "No. What's going on?"

I tell frank about the man in the outer office and he says, "Have your men hold him for questioning. I'll send a couple of my guys to pick him up."

I tell the Goons standing by in my office to hold him for questioning and one of them goes out of my office door and there is a loud scuffle.

With five big Androids on him, the phony Iron Wall Investigator is subdued and disarmed. Inside his brief case we find three bugs waiting to be planted in my office.

Looks like Kevin is proving to be more dangerous inside the prison than he was outside. As long as he's inside he can issue orders and we can't get at him.

I have to figure out how to put a stop to this nonsense. It's time to do some serious investigation around the airline explosion. If there were any Goons involved, there will be a record somewhere tying Kevin to the incident. I have to bring in Iron Wall Security and find out if they have any resources that we can use to unravel this mess.

I pick up the phone and call the President of the company again. I get Frank on the phone and we talk about the airline incident.

Frank says, "I can send you a team of computer experts to dissect the system history files. Now that I know what we're looking for, if there is anything to find, we'll find it."

I am grateful for the chance to get any information about the incident.

Frank also suggests, "I also have a line into the Transportation Safety Administration. We can get a full copy of the incident report for that day."

I am blown away with the news. "Thank you, Frank. I can't begin to tell you how much I appreciate hearing that."

Frank laughs and says, "You can let me know how much you appreciate it when you pay the bill."

I chuckle and think, "That's Frank. It's all about business."

The next morning I go over the phone logs with Frank at his office at Iron Wall Security. Having no one who can be trusted right now, it makes sense to keep this information away from my staff.

Frank and I go over the phone records and listen to a handful of phone conversations from the prison and some of the internal calls.

Frank smiles and asks, "If you were Kevin and have three people you have to count on to watch your back in a crisis, which three would that be?"

We both did a high-five and smiled. Both Frank and I knew who it had to be. There is an old rule in the investigations business that says, "Follow the money."

I say, "Al Akken, Vice President of Legal Services, Glen Posey, Vice President of Security and Phil Macklin, Vice President of Finance. They are the only three Senior Vice Presidents on the staff and the only three Vice Presidents on the Board of Directors. Glen Posey is the one who called up the Phony Iron Wall Security guy, Bill Blanchard and sent him to bug my office."

These three men own a piece of the business and stand to profit by eliminating me.

We go to the holding cell at Iron Wall Security and there sits Bill Blanchard. He has refused to tell us his name up to now, or who sent him.

I sit down and look at Bill. What's your name?" I ask point blank." He looks back at me and says, "Screw you!"

I smile and say, "This is where we left off yesterday, Bill. Your name is Bill Blanchard, right?"

He shoots me a defiant look, but doesn't respond.

I lean in and tell him, "We've treated you pretty well, Bill. Since yesterday you've enjoyed some good wholesome food. This morning you had eggs to order with bacon and toast with coffee. The holding cell is warm and has a nice bed with a ten inch thick mattress, an easy chair and a big screen TV."

Bill looks at me hard and says, "Jam it! You're not getting anything out of me."

I sit back in my seat and ponder the situation for a while and wink at Bill. "Not to worry my friend. We would never mistreat you. As a gesture of good will, I'm going to release you. You will be free as a bird. In fact I will have you driven back to your car at Farmer Industries in one of our limousines and released."

At this, Bill gives me a quizzical glance.

I continue, "I want you to be as comfortable as possible. But first, I need to make a phone call over to Glen Posey and ask him why you would come to my office in order to bug it. I will tell him that you came straight to me and, for a price, you would let me in on the whole deal including the fact that Glen hired you, Bill."

Bill starts to squirm a bit. I say, "I'm going to ask Glen what he paid you, because you said you would tell me everything if I offered to double it."

Bill has rivulets of sweat running down his face and his hands are trembling.

I say, "I'll be right back. This won't take long."

Bill starts to call after me, crying and begging me to stop. Bill says, "I'll tell you everything I know if you just don't do this."

I'm thinking Bill is like a scorpion. If you let him go in a fit of sympathy, he will turn right around and sting you.

I hate to do this, but I make a phone call over to Glen Posey and ask him, "Why would Bill Blanchard come to my office in order to bug it?" I tell him, "Bill came straight to me and, for a price; he offered to let me in on the whole deal including the fact that you hired him. Glen, what did you pay Bill? He said he would tell me everything if I double it, so I did. Do you have any questions, because I sure as hell have a few?"

Glen is silent for a moment and I swear I can hear him sweat.

Glen finally says, "I have no idea what you're talking about." Then the line goes dead.

The next day they find Bill Blanchard's body in the backroom of a warehouse. He had been shot and the only evidence was a 45 ACP shell casing on the floor in the corner.

An astute Detective carefully lifts the casing from the inside with a pencil and slides it into a brown paper bag. He says, "They say you have to match the casing with the gun, but that's not always true." The lab finds a thumb print on the outside of the brass casing that is matched to Glen Posey. Now Glen Posey is known to have loaded the gun that was used in the murder.

I mumble, "Even with all the Goons around, I guess Glen just wanted to do the job himself."

Nancy is back to work and lovelier than ever. She has perfect taste in clothing. I also notice a slight fragrance of flowers and the sparkle of delicate Belgian crystal earrings that perfectly match the understated Belgian crystal necklace.

I assign her to work with Frank from Iron Wall Security to work with his team of computer experts.

Frank gives me a wink on the way out the door.

I'm not sure what that's supposed to mean.

Chapter 4 Fight for the People

Two days later Frank from Iron Wall Security shows up with a briefcase full of papers and says, "I had a team of computer experts dissect the system history files. We found plenty of good stuff.

"No one suspected that the system would be analyzed for evidence.

"I also used my line into the Transportation Safety Administration to get a full copy of the incident report for the airline explosion."

I focus my interest on the airline incident report.

I ask Frank, "How in the hell can landing gear failures result in an airline explosion killing everyone aboard and everyone at the gate?"

Frank says, "On the surface it looks like a cover up on the part of the TSA, but in reality, the report turns out to be legitimate."

I start to read and discover that the fuel truck was parked just under the right wingtip of the aircraft when the right landing gear collapsed.

The right wingtip came down on the fuel truck and a spark either from the marker light or the friction between the wing metal and the truck metal ignited the fuel.

The wing fuel tank ruptured as well and the outcome was an explosion that took out the airliner, the fuel truck along with the gate.

Frank filled me in on the actual series of events.

He says, "It turns out that the TSA investigation was less than accurate as to the chain of events. Everything in the report is true, but they are mistaken about the order of events.

"The truck exploded first, and then the landing gear collapsed and ruptured the fuel tank which exploded and took out the airliner and the gate.

"No one on the fuel truck was in on the kill.

"They were after you, Gill."

I am amazed. I ask, "How did they plant the bomb on the fuel truck?"

Frank says, "You have to thank Nancy for uncovering that aspect of the plot. Farmer Industries is a diversified company. They own the fuel company that supplies the airport."

I look over at Nancy and she doesn't even seem to respond to the praise with a smile or a glance.

Frank pulls out a short stack of printouts and says, "Analysis of the banking and finance records reveal a lot about the events leading up to Bill Blanchard's attempt to bug your office.

"Bank and finance records show that Phil Macklin signed the check for Bill Blanchard, but best of all, Phil's phone records and recordings show that he negotiated the payment and wrote the check."

The thumb print on the brass shell casing, the internal company phone calls, the check signature, these may not hold up in a murder trial because they are somewhat circumstantial, but, they are grounds for termination.

Glen Posey, Vice President of Security and Phil Macklin, Vice President of Finance are both immediately terminated and have no further access to the building.

The next day my private cell phone rings and its Lieutenant Daggett, "Good afternoon Professor Bennett.

"We need to talk regarding some of the recent developments over at Farmer Industries. We can chat in your office or we can chat in mine, which will it be?"

I'm taken a bit off guard and ask, "Where did you get my cell phone number?"

Lieutenant Daggett responded, "I am calling on a pressing matter, Professor. In my opinion the murder of the consultant was somewhat open and shut.

"In fact I think it was far too premature. I have requested a thorough investigation by the Securities and Exchange Commission due to the number of changes in your high level management due to criminal activities. The more I delve into your operation, the more it leaves a sour taste in my mouth."

My patience begins to run out, "Lieutenant, the case is closed. All the evidence is in. You have your culprits.

"The personal improprieties of a handful of employees are no concern of yours.

"Unless you have a warrant or you wish to discuss an active case, you can leave me alone and stop poking your nose in our company business!

"By the way, none of the criminal activity was a matter for the Securities and Exchange Commission."

I abruptly closed my cell phone.

The only threat remaining in the company is Attorney Al Akken, the Senior Vice President of legal services. By eliminating the other two conspirators, I have tipped of Al Akken to my intentions. Now Al will be a double threat to my security. I need to find a way to isolate him from the situation.

Lawyers are generally the most difficult people to trap, because they tend to represent others, and don't tend to originate anything. We have combed every aspect of the situation, but none of the records implicate him in any of the activities.

For the moment, Al is busy defending Phil Macklin and Glen Posey. Phil and Glen are charged with conspiracy in the industrial espionage investigation stemming from the attempted bugging of my office.

I recommended that Al Akken defend the accused pair on the grounds that he is best qualified to protect them against the charges.

The pair naturally wants to put their interests first and agree that Al is the man for the job. The deal is sealed by a Circuit Judge and the stage is set for my next objective, to cut off Al Akken from the inner workings of the company.

The best way to isolate us from the wrath of Kevin Farmer and Al Akken is to cut a deal with an outside law firm called Bentley and Bentley, PC.

I downsized my entire law firm with the argument that they are too small to serve our future marketing objectives.

Once they were down to a manageable size, I eliminated the legal department completely.

As for Al Akken, I am arguing that his defense of the employees accused of espionage against my office represents a conflict of interest. He can't possibly defend them and serve my best legal interests at the same time.

Al Akken is put on an indefinite leave of absence. This should buy me time to figure out how to get rid of both Kevin and Al for good.

Nancy is exploring the legal landscape to find a law firm I can put on permanent retainer to work on issues surrounding the legalization of the Cure for use on humans.

All of this has really taken its toll on my ability to drive the company product strategy forward. My marketing department and I have a meeting to discuss the many facets of the problem and some possible solutions.

I tell the committee, "We are already providing miraculous cures for animals, which proves that the machine works.

"The rumor on the street is that it's not safe for human applications. The AMA along with the pharmaceutical industry gave joined forces to block the use of the machine along with insurance companies and other financial interests.

"We need to work around them and get to the grass roots public to make them aware that this is a viable solution for them. Any ideas on how we can make that transition?"

A bright young man near the end of the table speaks up, "We need to join forces with groups who already have the public's ear. Groups like the ASPCA and Right to Life along with those who are striving for political change.

"If we get these groups all lined up we can manipulate them and get to the general public on several levels.

"We want people to side with us. We don't care which of many reasons they might have."

I am impressed with the idea and tell him, "You are in charge of identifying which groups we want to affiliate ourselves with and how that will be accomplished."

Turning to Nancy I say, "Get that young man's name. I want him on my committee to capture the medicinal marketplace."

I ask again, "Any other ideas on how we can get this machine in the hands of people who can save human lives?"

Another person says, "Our problems are due mainly to the industrialized countries of the world. The industrial powers of the world have little political influence over the smaller countries. The smaller countries have no membership in the circus that drives the global economy.

"Let's pick out some countries that are susceptible to the idea of saving lives.

"Also there are those countries that have always either been at war with western philosophy or who are more bold in their acceptance of new technologies."

We need statistically conclusive data to base our campaign on, so I say to Human Resources, "I am ordering a new field office to be created in Nigeria.

"We don't know anything about the local legal requirements for medical equipment and practice there. Let's relocate Al Akken to head up the office as soon as he is back from administrative leave. I think his legal skills can help us determine the best way to comply with Nigerian law."

We set up a new office in the corporate suite labeled foreign acquisitions.

We begin staffing efforts to bring in people to serve on our staff from the target countries where we want to set up offices.

I proclaim, "We have to acquire some established buildings for our offices in the target countries. By saying established buildings, we don't have time to build new sites, or mess with build to suit deals.

"I want these offices functional within thirty days even if it results in paying a premium for the site."

I tell Nancy, "Order a meeting for me with Bentley and Bentley for next week. The subject is foreign markets and the legal requirements to enter into them.

"Also, I want to know what authority the government might have to block the export of our technology to counties who are not on the no trade list."

Shortly thereafter my phone rings and its Carmine Bentley. Car says, "I don't know if we can fit you in this week, Gill."

My immediate response is, "We're a high end account with a high end project. Time is of the essence. If you lack the resources to support our needs, I'll go elsewhere."

Car says, "Hold on Gill. I will do whatever I can to keep this account. What do you need?"

Now that I have his attention I answer, "I'm in a race with the government to get my product to market overseas. I want my products in place and functional before the government realizes what happened. There will be an attempt to stop me because the health care industry doesn't want this product used on humans."

There is a short pause and I hear Car sigh.

Next I tell him what I want to see, "I want a dedicated full time staff located here on site to drive this project. It will take about three people.

"I need your best Lawyer who is familiar with the project, a paralegal and a legal secretary who can type fast enough to get things out the door.

"I'm paying you a fat retainer. If it's not enough, let me know what you need, but keep it fair."

Car says, "The meeting will be set for first thing Monday morning at 8:00 AM. I'll have your staff there for you."

Once we're operating overseas our ability to protect our position in the market is up for grabs.

The use of the 3D chipset will create a barrier to entry into reproducing our design for The Cure.

We have purchased a warehouse in Switzerland because it is the crossroads to every country in the world from the USA to Iran and Nigeria. From this point we can ship anywhere in the world.

We've stepped up our production of the MRI/MRE chipset and have shipped two thousand units as of this month.

The 3D Chipsets, printed circuit boards and control consoles have shipped out to Switzerland through American Customs by conventional freight haulers. For the more difficult exports to Switzerland we have a large company yacht fully loaded with Goons ready to set sail as though going out for a party at sea.

The boat moves out to the twelve mile national control limit and meets with a freighter on the high seas where the cargo is transferred. The cargo transfers quickly because the Goons can each walk from the yacht to the freighter.

Even if the yacht is intercepted by the Coast Guard or Harbor Patrol, the Goons are just partying people, after all.

After one trip a day for a week, the full complement of cargo is aboard the freighter and it can depart.

The freighter makes the journey over almost to the Bay of Biscay where the transfer of Goons and material makes its way to our private company dock.

The Goons are not subjected to security screening because the French pleasure craft is a local sailing vessel.

The long trip is made simple by the fact that no provisions are required for the two thousand Goons, as they neither eat nor drink. It's made legal because the Goons are personal property, not people, so we're not smuggling people across any boarders without legal passports.

"They're not for sale, so we're not smuggling merchandise that are bought or sold, and therefore have nothing of value to declare to Customs. We might as well be sending my appliances to Europe to be used in my home there.

On the fourth trip out to the freighter, I return to find Lieutenant Daggett waiting for me at the dock.

I smile and say, "What a pleasant surprise. What can I do for you this evening, Lieutenant? Do you have a warrant, probable cause, any grounds to invoke the plain view doctrine?"

The Lieutenant doesn't seem to be bothered by my abrupt tone. He just smiles and says, "I'm not here on official business this time. I was boating off the coast and saw your yacht go by.

"A man has to take a little time out for himself once in a while so I thought I'd squeeze in a little fishing. Anyway, I couldn't help but notice that the yacht was sitting a bit low in the water on the way out from here."

I nod and say, "Yes, go on."

He points behind him at the building and says, "Just thought I'd stop in and say hello. Would you care for some fish?"

By this time I'm at wits end and respond, "You're fishing alright, but it's not for fish. What goes on here is none of your damned business. How can I make that clear?"

The Lieutenant continues to speak, "When you returned to the dock just now, it's obvious that your yacht is sitting high in the water. Drop anything off, did you?"

Now he has my attention. This guy is going to haunt me until he comes up with something. I quickly say, "Look, I have a hard day tomorrow. Excuse me if I don't see you out."

The Board of Directors is also traveling to Geneva to see the factory and meet Gunter, the new Plant Manager. The title Plant Manager is a bit of a misnomer because he is the only human working in Geneva.

The next morning Nancy and I rush to catch our flight to Switzerland via London Heathrow and on through Zurich. It was nice to have a little downtime in view of the fact that it was a bit difficult to sleep last night. Even the layovers were restful after the scramble to get materials over here. For a change I actually feel rested on arrival at Switzerland's Geneva Airport.

I have a brief wait for the company limo and the Gunter is sitting in the back of the car waiting for us. He thought we could save a little time if we talked on the way to our conference center in Geneva.

Gunter exchanges a few pleasantries and then he gets right down to business saying, "Since the defense of the factory and warehouse will be required, we decided to source all of our weapons and ammunition purchases from Israel to avoid the hassle of dealing with arms exports from the United States.

"We arm Goons with .440 caliber Israeli Arms Desert Eagles and Russian made AK47s."

I pause in my proverbial tracks for a moment and ask, "What do you think this is all about, Gunter? Are we saving mankind from the scourge of disease, or are we waging war?"

Gunter seems lost in thought for a moment, tapping his finger on the black leather armrest and laments, "What's the difference? We're in for a hell of a fight either way, aren't we?"

It's clear to me that Gunter is the best choice to drive my project over here.

I smile and say, "Yes. It's going to be a hell of a fight."

The limo glides to a stop in front of one of many apartment buildings we use as a makeshift office building in downtown Geneva. There are no signs on the apartment building to reduce the likelihood of anyone attempting to attack it.

We change the address for our meetings on a regular basis and never let the owners know the real purpose of the rental. We pay a premium for the apartment rentals on a one year basis.

At the meeting with our Board of Directors I say, "Our factory back in the states geared up for the production of the scanning chambers and began producing fully assembled chambers three months ago. When testing was completed, they were on the Swiss docks within ninety days.

"I want you each to see the factory in Switzerland first hand. While we do have process controls in place, the product is too complex to rely on statistical sampling as a means for quality control. Rather, we need quality assurance.

"Unlike most products, we can't use the statistical six sigma model introduced by Robert Deming. We have to do 100% functional testing. The Deming Management Model focuses on controlling the quality of the process in order to control the quality of the product. This is done through the monitoring of manufacturing control limits."

On the way from the apartment meeting to the factory, Gunter tells me, "Armed security is critical to our operation because of the exclusivity of the materials involved. Also, the pressures applied internationally make the factory and the management targets for political, military and mercenary attack."

Each of our cars are led and followed by limousines occupied by Goons. All twenty one limos are armored vehicles with run-flat tires.

I complement Gunter, "You have done a fine job of setting things up here. We have made a major investment in the project. We have to make it work.

"How are you doing in terms of getting target countries to open their borders to this service?"

Gunter is the nearest thing to a CEO over here because we have had to streamline the operation to make it move swiftly.

He says, "I have lined up meetings with the governments of Nigeria and Niger along with Zimbabwe. We have to make sure they represent no military threat to the United States.

"We are forced to focus on third world countries for the initial human medical demonstrations."

I agree and add, "Make sure you Stay away from Japan and stay away from China. They would welcome the service, but have too many financial interests in the American medical industry."

Our limo arrives at the factory in its remote location in the country. The fences are electrified with warning signs all around.

Robert Stetson

I look with surprise and say, "You would think this was Area 51 or something."

Gunter looks confused and says, "Area 51?"

I just let it pass.

We enter the building and I can't help seeing that it's scarred on the outside with bullet pocks in the concrete. One corner of the building's roof is blown away.

The inside is in good condition, but I have to ask, "What's with the damage to the outside of the buildings?"

As I meet with the management team again at Fibrin Industries, I can see it's fortunate that we were able to get essential product shipped before the American product export embargo is put in place. Of necessity, the factory and warehouse are wholly owned by a Swiss Limited Liability Corporation, so the US product embargo couldn't force a recall of the product sold before the embargo was put into effect. Product sold and removed from the books is exempt from the restriction.

Farmer Industries created Fibrin, LLC as an independent corporate body. The profits from the sales and marketing of services are put into a joint account with Farmer Industries who can then transfer the funds to America.

The American government can govern product exports, but they can't govern Swiss services or Swiss partnerships with American companies.

As we all enter the elevator Gunter explains, "We have had on the average of one to two attacks on our facility each month since we began working here. The warehouse and the factory buildings are decoys. The real operation is well underground in bunkers.

"We're actually overdue for another attack. People don't want us to build this product. The Swiss Government is providing Police protection, air cover and troops when the going gets tough."

I hesitate for a moment and then ask, "Who is attacking us?"

Gunter says, "We can't tell if it's a false flag operation or not. We see uniforms on the soldiers, but the captives don't even know who hired them."

I can't believe there is this much hell to pay over a product introduction."

Nancy perks up and asks, "Why are the Swiss putting up with our presence here?"

Gunter chuckles and says, "Taxes. Lots and lots of taxes based on the projected profits. We are greasing palms all the way from here to Nairobi and on to South Africa."

I smile and say, "We're not actually in it for the money right now, but if we can prove the machine is safe for humans and get a groundswell of support, we can make trillions of dollars in the long run.

"The money we make on one year of Cure Insurance in Africa alone will more than compensate us for this African seed project."

Gunter grunts and nods.

The elevator doors open and we step out into a hallway with a dozen Goons standing around with side-arms and assault rifles.

I can see the members of the Board are not used to working in a combat environment, but then who is?

At the end of the hall the room opens up into a fully operational assembly plant with chambers lined up for fifty feet. Each chamber is being fitted with electronics and then fully wired and tested.

Gunter says, "We don't have a source for about fifteen hundred lab rats with cancer, but we do have fifteen hundred lab rats with a virus strain we've injected.

"As they are cured, they can also be re-infected. It takes about two weeks for the incubation period before the rat can be reused for testing.

"To save on overhead, we trained some of the Goons to work in the assembly plant. They not only work for time on the recharging stations, but they also eliminate the security risk of outside labor. We sometimes forget they are machines and don't require food or sleep."

I am overwhelmed by my obvious lack of insight. I ask, "Why am I hiring people to work in my factories back in the United States? Think of the money and aggravation we could save, not to mention break time and vacation days if I used Goons more effectively."

The Assembly line grinds to a halt and the assembly workers all have guns in hand. There is a mass exodus to the stair wells.

Gunter urges us all into an elevator and we begin our assent to the surface. Gunter says, "There is no reason for the Goons to use the elevator. They don't mind climbing a few hundred stairs. I ordered the elevators to remain clear for humans and freight."

I'm hearing loud noises and explosions that are getting louder as we ascend. The doors open and its pandemonium.

Gunter has one hand in the small of my back and the other hand in the small of Nancy's back.

We're being propelled through a door into a large room across the hall.

I think we're on the ground floor, but the entire wall ahead is wall to wall glass from floor to ceiling and it looks as though we're up about four stories off the ground.

"What the hell is this?" I inquire.

Gunter laughs and says, "Welcome to virtual reality. We are still three stories underground. The glass wall is a huge liquid crystal display and the door you passed through has a sliding, armored blast door covering it.

That's why we have to hurry. I don't want to be half way through the door when it closes"

Outside I can see soldiers massing into groups and attacking the factory. Then I notice the Goons painted in bright orange jump suits with their leather utility belts and the huge Desert Eagle .440 side arms.

The attacking human soldiers are advancing cautiously using cover every chance they get, but the Goons are fighting like ants.

I say to Gunter, "They swarm without regard for their safety. No human can be so single minded in the attack as to not care whether or not they live or die."

Gunter smiles and says, "As I said earlier, we forget they are machines."

I ease back into one of the puffy leather chairs. It's so comfortable.

A Goon approaches and offers me a drink. I say, "Yes, I'll have a scotch and water."

Gunter sits down by me saying, "I'll have the same."

Two minutes later we are served with our scotch and water. The Goon made them triples and places a bowl of peanuts and a bowl of chips along with a bucket of ice between the glasses, just in case we want to cool them.

Gunter winks and says, "We train our Goons well."

The battle rages on, but not much longer. By the time we have half-finished our drinks the scene has settled and we are victorious. Jeeps of Goons are scouting the area looking for stragglers or soldiers hiding on the property.

A big flatbed truck is hustling around and picking up the Goon bodies that have ceased to function due to massive damage.

Gunter explains, "They will be transported to the refurbishing center for repair or to be parted out."

I say, "Parted out?"

Gunter says, "Used for parts to repair or rebuild other Goons. We're comfortable now, let's all relax and finish our drinks."

I can hear the rumble of the blast door rolling back into its hiding place.

The glass wall turns into a deep sea scene complete with squids and hump back whales. Just for a moment I thought I heard a hump back whale song.

The Goon is back with two more drinks and a bowl of popcorn.

Gunter looks at me and says, "We train them too well. Would any of you like a pizza or a bowl of spaghetti? Our attendant is an excellent cook"

We have dinner and leave the comfort of the war room. Gunter takes me around to show me the storage facility and Goon refurbishing center.

I'm amazed at the process for growing artificial skin. It looks and feels real and has the pours and hairs in place.

I have to ask, "Gunter, what happens to the human soldiers that are left on the field out there?"

Gunter says, "They take them away. We are lucky that even the mercenaries have a code of conduct that states there will be no one left behind. We haven't bothered to take any prisoners this time."

I puzzle over the comment regarding the decision not to take prisoners and ask, "What do you mean you didn't bother to take prisoners?"

Gunter says, "The battle was too small and too short to bother.

The Swiss Police come and if there are any prisoners or any uncollected bodies, they deal with them.

There is the inevitable questioning of witnesses and collection of evidence along with the standard scolding for disturbing evidence because we removed our damaged Goons."

Gunter is becoming increasingly aggravated, but goes on, "We are forced to remind the Police that they breeched our security and attacked our buildings and equipment. The attack was unprovoked.

"We can't allow our trade secrets to be removed for examination. The Goons are simply our proprietary trade secret computer hardware and software that are damaged in the attack."

Nancy rarely speaks, but comments on Gunter's remark saying, "I feel good that Gunter is protecting our trade secrets."

I realize that Geneva Switzerland is nine hours ahead of the time zone back in Silicon Valley.

I have to call my office there two hours after we close our offices here, while here in the Geneva area.

I tell Nancy, "It is important for me to talk with our Human Resources Manager about converting our workforce over to Goons. Also, I want to hire a World markets Vice President to work the evening shift because if I have to be available in the new world market, it means I will get less sleep than ever."

Minutes later, Nancy hands me the phone and I'm on the line with our stateside office.

I tell Human Resources, "Hire Dr. Martin Gold as our new Senior Vice President in charge of World Markets to deal with these conference calls in the wee hours of the morning if you can get him on board."

When Monday morning arrives, I am eager to get back to my office in the United States.

Nancy and I board a flight to America via London Heathrow and on through New York where I connect to San Jose.

It is imperative that I meet with the members of the Board when they return from Geneva, to introduce them to our new Vice President, Martin Gold at a catered reception dinner. Martin Gold is sufficiently important to our mission to warrant a catered dinner to mark the occasion.

Dinner and the meeting are followed up with a one on one meeting with Martin to bring him up to date on our foreign operations. In our discussion I spoke of the attacks on the factories and the offices.

Martin asks, "Why can't we just let the Swiss Police deal with the criminals?"

I explain, "Because they aren't equipped to deal with combat forces. These criminals are mercenaries, not just thugs. We have had to build an army to combat them and the Swiss Police let us defend our property, as is the right of any Swiss Citizen."

Martin nods, and then asks, "Why haven't you patented the 3D Chipset or the Cure?"

I smile and tell him, "Because a patent requires full disclosure, but trade secrets are protected by law.

"Also, I don't want the world to know about the Goons. We have a contract with the armed forces for androids that look somewhat human, but not as human looking as ours. The only difference is in the appearance.

"Our shipments to Switzerland aren't illegal because we pay no tariff on exports, just our imports."

I'm thinking Martin is fantastic.

Martin tells me, "I am studying the past five years of company history to get a good understanding of who we are and what has transpired.

"While going over the last year of sales, I noticed that your Senior Vice President in charge of legal services, Al Akken signed off on the contract for the sale of pleasure-droids for the escort industry."

I recoiled and blurted out, "Aside from being immoral, I regard the nature and intent of the contract as being illegal and grounds for dismissal.

"No one can differentiate between our androids and a real person. I never knew we were in any segment of the entertainment industry."

Martin Faxes me the list of sales with contract dates and dollar amounts. Many of the customers are in the areas of the world where we are forbidden to sell potentially militaristic technology. The sales contract violates our export restrictions.

As an Attorney, I would expect Al to know this.

This phone call is a mixed blessing. I have to notify the military of the breach. My only saving grace is that all of the sales occurred before I came on board with Farmer Industries.

There will be export fines to pay and the company will be put under strict observation, but the good news is that Kevin Farmer and Al Akken will be behind bars for a very long time.

Four men in black and wearing those stereotypical sun glasses showed up in the lobby the next morning.

I understand they went to Al Akken's residence and took him away in handcuffs.

Right on the heels of the men in black's arrest of Al Akken were the auditing accountants with a warrant to review our records going back to the day we signed an agreement with the government.

The Justice department gave me and Farmer Industries a break because I had promptly reported the incident.

Robert Stetson

Chapter 5 Hardship and Morality

It just seems like the world is digging deep into my business at a time when I'm trying to keep a low profile.

Those two thousand Goons I gave to the Swiss company, Fibrin Industries, to protect the factory and warehouse have shown up on their inventory. They showed up on the manufacturing list, but there were no sales associated with them. Since they were transported out of the country on my yacht, there were no shipping records either.

I did manage to anticipate the problem and put a few of them on a scrap list. They are listed as destroyed. They are destroyed in battles that rage over there in Switzerland at Fibrin Industries.

The factory for manufacturing escort androids is shut down and those people unfortunately have to find work elsewhere.

There are a lot of angry people who can't get new escort androids or service on the product any longer.

Local authorities around the world are baffled by the fact that these androids are machines violating the law and not accountable for the way they are used.

They can't just be handcuffed and prosecuted for prostitution because prostitution is a human crime. These androids fall into the class of big sex toys.

It comes as no surprise that the front desk in the lobby calls up to my office and tells me. "Lieutenant Daggett is on his way up to see you, sir."

As quickly as the phone call came there is a disturbance in the hallway outside my outer office door. I walk out to see what the noise is all about, but I already know. Three of the Goons have Lieutenant Daggett in their grip and he is wild with rage.

With a wave of my hand the Goons release the Lieutenant and step back. He goes for his weapon, but I say, "No one here has threatened you in any way. My assistants have simply stopped you from trespassing."

I smile and extend my hand in the direction of the Lieutenant saying, "Lieutenant Daggett. What brings you so rudely to my door?"

He looks as though he has worked himself into a blind rage.

While straightening his wrinkled clothes, he shouts, "If it's the last thing I do, you're going down Bennett!"

After a brief pause he regains his composure and pulls out that damned little note book and stubby pencil.

His voice is gruff as he speaks asking, "When was it that you actually began your employment here at the factory? You had a contract with Mr. Farmer and your employment began when you signed the document, but you took charge of the company at one point, didn't you?"

Nancy starts to speak, but I signal her to be still.

Moving in closer to the Lieutenant, I sternly reply, "Is this in reference to an open investigation?

"Where do you get the authority to barge in here without a warrant and start shaking me down?"

Daggett smiles slyly and says, "I'm conducting a preliminary investigation to determine if a more in depth investigation is needed. It's a fact finding visit to determine probable cause."

I signal the Goons to stand by and tell the Lieutenant, "I already furnished all this information to the Federal authorities.

"If you look at the information they have then there is no reason for you to be here.

"If you don't have access to the information then you're out of your jurisdiction. Either arrest and charge me with something or get out."

Looking over at Nancy I see her on the phone.

She gives the Lieutenant a dirty look and then says to me, "I have Attorney Car Bentley on the line. He is on his way to speak to the Lieutenant about a charge for harassment."

Robert Stetson

Lieutenant Daggett puts the pencil and booklet away and nods.

He turns and walks toward the door and says, "That's all for now, Bennett. I think I have everything I need from you."

Now my office is being flooded by phone calls from around the world demanding product and repairs on their recreational androids.

This distresses me because they are interfering with my primary goal to get the Cure on the market.

The phone rings and its Frank over at Iron Wall Security and he sounds rather stern, "Gill. My people tell me you shut down the factory in Omaha making recreational escorts.

"They also say you are reneging on contracts to customers. These are people you don't want to cross."

I start taking about the military non-disclosure agreement and the export restrictions placed on us by the government.

I also tell him, "The contracts are legal on the surface, but the trade restrictions trump any contract we might have signed."

Frank's tone doesn't change and he says, "I feel for you, Gill. You're in a bad situation here.

"The medical and insurance industry wants to kill you.

"Every criminal organization in the world who deals in human trafficking and the sex trades wants to kill you.

"Kevin Farmer and Al Akken both want you dead for blowing the whistle on them, not to mention the billions of dollars they stood to make on the pleasure droids, and to put the cherry on the cake.

"Your activities overseas have captured the interest of the CIA because the lives you stand to save with your Cure machine means billions of dollars being paid out in Social Security to elderly people who would have died if it weren't for you.

"Gill, you're raising hell with the actuarial tables of every welfare, Social

Security, and entitlement programs around the world."

I am exasperated by the magnitude of the problem and ask, "So what would you have me do? I'm between a rock and a hard place. Any suggestions on how we can deal with this situation?"

Frank says, "I already have a team of my best men on their way over there.

"Sit tight and don't meet with anyone until you check with me. I want to screen everyone who shows up on your door, or who you have appointments with.

"I want you to FAX me your calendar."

Now I have a concern with Frank's desire to see my calendar.

Maybe I'm getting a bit paranoid, but then, if everyone is out to kill me I'm not actually paranoid, am I?

I'm wondering whether Frank is spying on my progress in getting the Cure to market so he can report to someone on my activities, or maybe setting me up for a hit in a convenient location.

Then I'm wondering if Frank is simply looking for the resources he will require to keep me alive. Things are getting a bit bleak when you have to question the intentions of the very people you hired to keep you alive.

I decide to keep my calendar private for now. Aside from surrounding myself with people I trust, there isn't much more I can do.

Cure machines are shipped from Switzerland to our test Centers in Africa where they will be set up in clinics for use on treating humans. The shipments are made under heavy guard. The means of delivery and the schedules are secret.

Cure centers around Nigeria and Niger along with Zimbabwe are opened amid the protest of the United States. They welcome the service.

The lines of broken people with their broken spirits are long. We create waiting centers because the strain of standing in line is far too hard for most. At the waiting centers we take their name, age and other information. We collect their vital signs and when we must, we establish a triage for the center.

People pay what they can afford which is often nothing at all.

Nancy and I book a trip to the areas on board our Farmer Industries Boing 747 over to Heathrow Airport in London and then go the rest of the way to Africa by way of our Lear Jet.

The smaller airplane can land on shorter runways and uses a more conventional fuel than the jumbo jet.

Nancy has been a constant comfort to me in the most trying of times.

Westerners have been accustomed to hearing about the depravity found in the so called third world countries. They actually have some of the finer four star hotel accommodations.

Nancy and I have become an item and spend our evenings together, sharing a room, sharing good times and sharing our lives.

I feel that my life has become a blend of ecstasy and stark terror. Being the target for assassination can intensify every element of your attitude about life in general.

On our way from Niger to Nigeria our convoy stops momentarily to allow a mule driven cart to pull aside so we can pass.

Our armored vehicle is not built for comfort to the extent that our Limousines back home are. The air conditioning works fine, but the ride is stiff and can jar the passengers around quite a bit.

It's hot, humid and the sun is blindingly bright in the areas between where the road passes through thick overgrown trees and foliage.

Our convoy is led by a buzz truck that has vertical spinning blades that cut away the overgrowth on either side. The buzz truck is followed by a bull dozer, pushing the debris aside to form a smoother road. Roads not travelled in the previous seventy two hours can begin to be overgrown in the tropical heat and moisture.

Camped out on either side of the road there are the native people who have made their lives in the jungle thickets.

As we wait for the wagon to clear the way for our convoy there is a disturbance just behind our follow vehicle.

I hear an explosion and some automatic gunfire.

There are swarms of attacking men with guns all around us.

The twelve Goons from the lead and follow cars are engaging them in hand to hand combat.

Something I never really considered before is the fact that while Goons do breathe and eat and drink and eliminate the air, food and fluids they consume, they do not process any of it.

The Goons are electrical. They are immune to toxic gas and poisons and can't be drowned or suffocated. The armored vehicles are sealed against the outside air, so we are unaware that there is a plume of defensive poisoned gas bursting from each of our vehicles.

The swarms of attacking soldiers disperse quickly once they realize they can't fight us on our own terms.

The Goons are relatively unscathed, but I see skin pulled aside on a couple of them that reveals the titanium metal skull underneath.

One Goon has an eye out and the socket is looking like a car with the headlight missing, but with a red glow in the back of the small cavern. It's not a gruesome sight as one might imagine, but rather strange because the injured Goon is smiling.

I say to Nancy, "We have to work on that grinning problem. It still gives me the willies."

My android guide is calm offering Nancy and me a beverage or a snack while we wait to proceed.

Looking at the chaos that erupted all around us, I had to ask, "Was that a band of highwaymen looking to rob us?"

Our guide says, "No, Gill. Those soldiers were after you. They are soldiers of fortune hired by one of many governments, companies or organizations that want you dead at any price. You have become a much sought after celebrity.

Nancy and I are taking more of these short company armored vehicle convoys to each of the clinics where we visit the waiting, treatment and recovery centers.

We see people at the waiting centers that are in pain. They are hungry and they are destitute. These people have lost all hope and have been ignored by society. There are mothers whose babies won't live past morning without the Cure.

At the end of each day Nancy and I weep in the privacy of our room under the strain of all the needless death and dying.

The pain and suffering are taxing my inner strength, but Nancy seems stronger somehow. She gives me hope saying that, "One day the world will be a nicer place.

Our grief is not for of those we saved because they came to us, but because so many innocent souls who didn't make it in time to be renewed."

I reach over and take her hand telling her, "Many nights while sitting in my room, I have often wondered what it must be like to be filthy rich, not in spite of, but because of the agony of others.

When is enough pleasure, riches and power enough? When are the riches enough to stop taking for yourself, and let all the sick and poor around you have a small taste of life?"

We are a year into the project and nearly every person in the area where we placed our Cure clinics is healthy.

African statistical evaluations reveal that the Cure has had none of the adverse after effects on the health of the population that are being touted by the governments, insurance or medical industries of the world.

There has not been a single contraindication resulting from our treatments. The cure rate has been 100% effective while treating any of the viruses or bacteria in our databases.

Being in Africa is having a positive impact on the range of illnesses we treat.

We come across a myriad of new strains of bacteria and viruses that exist only in this part of the world so our data base is being improved.

We notice there is a major increase in the local population statistics caused by the dramatic increase of lives we save. We fully expect to see that.

We also know that the statistics on the median age of the population will be drifting upward because the majority of the people we save are the elderly who would not normally have otherwise survived the illness.

A society is based on a number of balanced statistics, so upsetting any of the numbers ranging from population, demographics or economic factors will have a profound effect on all of the other elements of the society.

As is the rule in any balanced system, gains in any area result in losses in other areas.

The dependence of so many elderly people who are alive and unable to contribute to the welfare of the economy is resulting in an upside down economic disaster.

The ratio of working to long retired people is beginning to tip the scales, severely impacting the quality of life and eventually promising to cause severe widespread economic collapse in Africa.

Between the closing of the escort segment of the business and my African campaign, the company revenues are taking a nosedive.

In the beginning the problem of economic decline was mainly in the United States because of the proliferation of programs designed to aid the elderly. The elderly population is growing rapidly. The Cure machine is only promising to aggravate the economic situation.

Now the economic decline is spreading around the globe as the world begins to grapple with the growing disparity between the working class and the longer living retirement community.

My VP of Finance visits my office with disturbing news about the restructuring of the world economy.

He tells me, "Now that the European currency has been converted to the Euro and the African currency to the Afro there is a move on to consolidate the North and South American currencies as well."

I'm concerned because over time the consolidation of the world monetary system will result in a consolidation of the world governments. The consolidation of the world governments will ultimately result in the consolidation of the world's justice system, laws and customs.

I shake my head in disbelief and tell him, "We had better get things moving quickly. If we don't soon get the proof we need that the Cure is safe for use on humans, we will never get the chance."

Nancy frowns and says, "We had better get our statistics together and get moving on the problem of conducting clinical trials in the United States. If we can prove that the Cure is perfectly safe and 100% effective the only objection left would be political."

I tell my secretary, "Arrange a special meeting of all department heads for tomorrow and have them bring their wives, husbands or significant others.

"Make it a catered dinner with wine and the whole nine yards. I want a live band. Make the music theme something conservative."

It's nearly lunchtime and I take Nancy to a particularly special restaurant where we have candlelight dinner with the finest cuisine.

I have reserved a special table in a quiet corner in a balcony and the soft candlelight plays across her face.

As I gaze deep into her intense blue eyes, she sighs and says, "Yes, I will marry you, Gill."

It throws me completely off guard. My composure is somewhat broken and I stammer for a moment.

"How did you know?" I ask.

Her smile grew softer and she says, "Oh, Gill. I'm so sorry. I've ruined everything haven't I?"

Now I pull out the ring and smile, "No, Nancy. You haven't ruined anything, but how did you know?"

She spreads her fingers on top of the table and I slip the ring on. She looks at the ring and then at me and I can see she is in ecstasy.

Her voice is like velvet as she speaks, "When you love someone, you can almost have an entire conversation without speaking.

"I knew what you were thinking when you ordered the meeting with all department heads and then made it such a special event."

She is right, of course. I would never have had the band, the wine nor had everyone bring their special partners unless I had a life changing announcement to make.

Nancy toyed with her fork and asks, "What if I had said no?"

I chuckle and say, "I knew you would say yes, but had you said no, it would have been a special appreciation dinner for the staff. Sadly, most of them will be let go when I announce the downsizing of the company in order to complete the changeover to the android work force."

I decide to put off telling the bad news to the staff until Nancy and I have been married next month and then taken our thirty nine day whirlwind honeymoon vacation.

Nancy is an orphan so she has no family. Her friends are all employees of Farmer Industries.

She told me, "My mom and dad passed away and I have no family to speak of. My friends are few because my life has always been about my work, which is somewhat controversial.

Needless to say it will be a small formal wedding."

I say, "Don't feel bad, honey. Being estranged from the university and with conflicting business relationships, my side of the church won't be overflowing either."

The thing that most disturbs me is that both my Best Man and the man who gives Nancy away will have to be Goons.

We have decided to dispense with the crowd of weeping Goons in the audience for effect. It just wouldn't make it all seem that much cozier.

The caravan of big black armored Limousines full of Goons leaving the church somehow spoils the free spirited atmosphere we are trying to create.

News comes in of an attack on our Zimbabwe clinic where the data for the last year is being compiled. The satellite uplink is destroyed so the data is unavailable for now.

Our data center in Omaha is put on alert to receive raw data from Niger and Nigeria as soon as possible.

Nancy and I are on board the company 747 in a matter of minutes and on our way to London for the connection with our Lear Jet which is standing by.

Food and coffee for the flights are kept on standby for just such an emergency, so the flight schedule isn't hampered by the need for provisions.

The jumbo jet makes haste across the Atlantic and touches down at Heathrow Airport.

Our Limo meets our airplane and transfers us to the Lear, which is already warming up on the tarmac.

By the time we arrive in Nigeria the sun was just coming up so it's a blinding glare low in the sky. The air is thick with humidity. The heat is stifling. God I hate the heat.

The usual convoy of Goons and armored vehicles move swiftly toward the clinic and the roads are open and well maintained.

If we have to go to Niger it will mean traveling that overgrown dirt road where we were attacked on our last visit.

Our strategy is to keep our mission working out of Nigeria where we are more mobile and better equipped.

We arrive in Nigeria to find Goons running in all directions. There is gunfire and helicopters are streaking in from over the jungle to fire their missiles, destroying the village and clinic.

A section of the ground opens in the road and we are descending into a downward sloping tunnel leading to an underground facility.

The driver tells us, "This is our bunker. We will be safe here."

Nancy wants to know, "Where is the data from the Cure Study?"

The driver doesn't respond. The doors open and we are escorted to a room with a full lounge.

The power reclining black leather chairs are big and soft. Attending Goons wait on us, providing food and beverages.

A man enters the room and introduces himself, "I am Dr. Emerson.

"We heard about the loss of data over in Zimbabwe. It was distressing news, but the good news is that we have a full underground computer complex here and the data from Niger and Nigeria are both safe.

"We're compiling the results right now. We have the data from Zimbabwe also, but it isn't complete yet, so we decide it is inconclusive."

The room trembles on occasion when a loud thundering sound is heard.

Dr. Emerson looks up toward the ceiling and says, "Don't be concerned. You are in a bunker thirty feet underground. The bunker is on a spring loaded platform that moves to absorb the shock of a direct hit."

We move to a large soft black leather sofa in the corner of the room and Nancy curls up next to me with her head resting on my fury chest.

I stroke her soft hair and look down at her. Her eyes meet mine and they are deep blue and hauntingly beautiful.

She looks so delicate, like a flower in the rain.

I kiss her forehead and pull her warm body close against me. She seems so vulnerable and innocent.

I love her so much it pains me to have brought her to this terrible place.

Robert Stetson

After a couple of hours Dr. Emerson arrives back in the room and says, "We have succeeded in transferring all of the data to your Omaha facility including the inconclusive information from Zimbabwe.

"They have confirmed receipt, so everything is fine. Everything topside is completely destroyed, but under the circumstances there will be no need to rebuild. Our job is done here."

I am struck by the lack of concern, or even a reference to all the people who were destroyed along with the village and the clinic.

I ask, "What of all the people? Were there any survivors? Do they need aid? It's our fault they are in the middle of this mess."

Dr. Emerson looks at me with a puzzled expression and answers, "I am only concerned with the project data. I am not concerned about the people. They are merely individual data points in our statistical analysis. The analysis is completed."

Now I understand why the whole damned team here seems unconcerned with anything other than the data.

He continues to speak saying, "There are no humans assigned to these projects in Africa.

"Surely, you must have realized that this project flies in the face of every government and business agency on the planet.

"Sir, did you honestly believe there would be no collateral damage here?"

I am dumfounded to discover just how aware these androids are. He seems to understand the entire global concept from the test data to the socioeconomic implications. He also seems to lack any understanding of the reason why I created the machine.

"How can you grasp the entire concept of the study, and yet feel nothing about the outcome with regard to human life?" I ask.

He looks at me with steely eyes and says, "Unlike you, my task is clear.

"You waste your time stoking the hair of your companion.

"You waste your time discussing people who are no longer living.

"Unlike you, Professor Bennett, I do not waste my time.

"I do not emote."

The door opens and a Goon steps in.

He says, "Professor Bennett. Your car is ready.

"The area is safe for your exit to the airport."

I almost said, "Thank you."

Then I remember they have no feelings. What would be the point?

Nancy gets up from the sofa and says to the Goon, "Thank you."

If people are going to be wearing medical smocks and dealing with the public, perhaps I need to have the engineering staff revisit the need for the Goons to at least feign concern for human life.

In our absence from the United States our wedding has been planned right down to the singer, organ music and the cake. It will be spectacular.

I had no idea that Farmer Industries has a costume department. I guess when you make thousands of androids and turn them loose from the factory; you would want them fully clothed. Each android is dressed in the appropriate costume for their programming, to include soldiers and attendants.

For our wedding, the bridesmaid's costumes, the beautiful wedding gown, the tuxes and other special clothing are easily created.

Farmer Industries has drivers and pilots that are human because they must be licensed. I suppose the drivers and pilots could be androids if we cared to treat them as "undocumented aliens." Funny, as I think of it, Androids being called "undocumented aliens" would be accurate because they are in the country legally.

Androids might be entitled to be licensed if I documented them by getting them a Social Security card, but then, they have no birth certificate. I would still have to have them legally documented by the Department of Immigration to get them a legal Social Security Card and then get them issued a license.

In the end, I guess whether you choose to call them illegal or undocumented doesn't matter. They are illegal and have to be documented by the Department of Immigration to work legally.

I'll just stay with the human drivers and pilots. It's easier.

The blood test and wedding license were all taken care of. The company doctor did the blood test results and the Lawyers have been given Power of Attorney granting them signatory authority to get the licenses and make arrangements. The wedding is on for next month. Nancy and I are so happy.

Calls are coming in from TV studios wanting me to be on the air for a debate with the Surgeon General's office to discuss the statistical results we received from Niger and Nigeria.

The media is referring to the project as the "Nigerian Experiment."

Reports are indicating that the results are premature, unsubstantiated or inconclusive depending on which news report you're listening to.

I agree to discuss the data on the news in order to get the facts out to the people.

The show is to air next week and I have a full team working to prepare the information I'm scheduled to deliver on the show tomorrow.

I have a small staff of people just to answer the phones and ward off the calls that are pouring in.

Reporters are deluging my home and office with calls.

Nancy and I haven't been home since I agreed to do the show because there is a large contingency of reporters on the lawn.

We are staying in my luxury office suite in the underground bunker here at work.

The street is crowded with TV News vans and their satellite dishes.

I mutter in desperation, "Don't they think I have anything better to do than discuss this issue right now? I have to prepare for the program tomorrow. They seem to want exclusive information now."

Security has informed me that the media is crowding the lobby of the building and trying to get on the elevators.

I order a large team of security officers in uniform to clear the reporters from the lobby and lock the outer doors.

The elevators are shut down and guards are posted in the stair wells.

The Police are called but don't respond. They say the press has every right to attempt to contact me and businesses are considered public buildings, so the press is not trespassing.

One of the Police Officers actually says, "They are only press-passing."

The remark seems to cause Nancy to smile. I don't think it was funny.

The crowds are nearly impassible as people have a clear vision of Nancy and me as we try to work our way toward the company Limo.

Security is a nightmare with so many people out to kill me and so many people straining to breach the security lines.

The Police are no help at all, as usual. They call this a civil matter citing the fact that the sidewalks and streets are public areas.

The convoy of Goon Limos departs from Farmer Industries on their way to the news studio to deliver Nancy and me.

Then there is a disturbance and shots ring out.

Four men push the crowd aside and a fifth presses forward with a bazooka pointed at our Limo.

There is a whooshing sound and the Law Rocket streaks forward finding its mark.

The Limo explodes in flame and there is nothing left but a huge fireball.

People all around are still being shot by the assassins or have been injured by flying shrapnel.

Ambulances, Fire and Police rush to the scene.

The killers use the mass hysteria to escape the scene.

Fortunately, Nancy and I decide to stay behind to watch from the eighth floor conference room. We are warned that there will be an attempt on my life today.

It isn't wise to put yourself in a certain place at a certain time when there are so many assassins waiting to take your life.

The silver windows go floor to ceiling and wall to wall, so we have a perfect view of the street below. From the outside the windows look like a solid mirror covering the entire face of the building.

Part of our preparation for future public appearances is the manufacture of Gill and Nancy clones. They are coming off the assembly line like Ken and Barbie dolls. We have thirty of the lookalike androids for each of us. The two androids in the Limo on the street below are decoys.

The cost of security is killing us. It reminds me of the security craze of the twenty first century when every aspect of the transportation industry along with every public building in the country was shrouded in the tightest possible security.

There was a fear of terrorism that generated an enormous security industry. Security is unlike any other enterprise because it creates no commercial value. America poured all of its resources into protecting people from the boogie men.

The United States almost went bankrupt before it realized that the terrorists weren't trying to kill anyone. They were trying to create such a wall of fear that we would destroy ourselves. We nearly did by bankrupting the entire country.

The news special is rescheduled for a secret time and place. The most secure place is inside our office building basement bunker.

We schedule it for tomorrow, but we don't notify the news that Nancy and I are still alive. Not just yet. We have more to do before we can risk having anyone know we're still on the job.

The TV news programs are reporting the chaos that followed our alleged attempt to go to the studio. There are telescopic cameras there from every major news network. The mayhem is recorded from every possible angle and from their news helicopters overhead. The Anchormen and Anchorwomen bemoan our passing.

We are now on the cover of every major media in the country. The word is that I was the last great hope of the average person who needed a lifesaving cure. There are candlelight vigils, midnight masses and flags fly at half-staff as the nation morns my untimely passing.

Nancy and I sip our drinks in the comfort of my bunker. The media knows it has an interview, but they don't realize it's with me.

I casually mention, "The attempted assassination may have been the best thing that ever happened to our cause.

"With me as a martyr and people believing that I could have saved the world, my message will get more attention that it ever otherwise would have, don't you think?"

Nancy nods, studies her glass, and says, "As hard as things have been, things are starting to look up.

"I just hope they don't say you staged the whole thing to get attention."

"I hadn't thought of that" I say.

Seems there are always two ways of looking at everything.

This could get hairy very soon if we don't get something positive to happen.

The time has arrived for the company interview with the TV News team. They were told they would be interviewing the VP of Marketing.

The news crew is escorted down to my bunker and they appear elated to see me alive. Amy Kravis is the news anchor. She is beside herself with exuberance. "Does anyone know you're still alive?" she asks.

Robert Stetson

We assure her that she has an exclusive story here.

Along with an exclusive interview and debate with the Surgeon General we planned a tour of the factory and warehouse if they are interested. I think if they see the product during manufacture they will see it's real.

"Would you care to see the manufacturing process?" I ask.

For purposes of this program, we have put all twenty nine remaining android copies of Nancy and me away and out of sight for the tour.

The 3D Chipset and android programs are too sensitive a topic for public broadcast. We can allow the goons to continue working while we are on the tour because they look entirely human.

We can't identify them as Goons because the confidentiality agreement with the military forbids it.

Amy Kravis says, "Yes. We would love to see your factory and warehouse, but I will have to clear it with my Production Manager. Can we do it on another visit?"

I nod agreement.

The debate with the Surgeon General is almost ready except for the presence of my Statistics Analysis team. They have the past treatment records and performance numbers.

We also have a film clip showing the procedure in progress. It's a young African Boy with terminal cancer on his death bed. He looks slim and pale with sallow cheeks and vacant eyes. The film clip also includes footage of the same young boy shot one month after treatment. He is robust and healthy. He has gained a lot of weight and is dancing with his tribal brothers. His face is healthy and he has bright shiny eyes.

We intend to show this film clip during the debate. It should have a positive impact on the viewers.

There is so much excitement at the moment about me being alive that Amy Kravis has been given the green light for a live TV News Special.

The show is preempting regular broadcasting and I have had no real time to prepare for being thrust into the public eye, but WATT TV wants to get their exclusive news broadcast out to the public.

Amy holds the microphone up to my face and asks me, "Gill, how is it you're here alive with Nancy when we saw the two of you get into the Limo just seconds before the terrible explosion?"

I smile for the camera and say, "Well, Amy. We obviously weren't in the car at the time the rocket actually hit the vehicle."

Amy starts making faces and small pumping motions with the mike to indicate that I should keep talking.

I continue to speak, "That's all I can really say about that."

Nancy says, "We aren't at liberty to discuss that right now.

"We are alive and well and hope everyone watching will write their Congressman about getting the Cure approved for humans."

We are directed to stand behind two podiums while the station takes a short commercial break.

The podiums are marked, one with the government seal and mine with the Farmer Industries, LLC logo.

Amy turns to the Surgeon General and says, "Are you ready to discuss the Cure for the public, Sir?"

The Surgeon General says, "Yes I am. There is a lot of hype and misconception about this machine.

"My office has looked into the benefits and long term effects of the treatments. We're convinced that it's hazardous to your health and not fit for use on humans."

I turn to him and say, "How can you talk about long term effects when a person has only days to live? Isn't that a bit short sited?"

He retorts with, "We haven't seen one shred of evidence that even suggests this machine of yours actually works on humans."

I tell the Production Manager it's time to roll the film clip where the young boy is miraculously cured of terminal cancer. The film clip runs and takes all of about five minutes to complete.

I start to feel confident and say, "As they always say, 'seeing is believing' and 'the camera doesn't lie'."

He responds with, "That's usually true, Gill, but liars do cam.

For instance, we saw you killed in a Limo explosion. If cameras don't lie, then you're not here right now."

I respond, "You saw the film clip with the young boy being critically ill with terminal cancer. Are you saying he wasn't sick in one scene and well in the next?"

He says, "I saw one of two things. Either the boy was well and then he became ill and you switched the segments to make it look as though he was cured, or those were two different boys."

I have proof that my machine works, but he keeps rationalizing as to how the evidence is false. My statistician takes over the argument by presenting his statistical proof that the machine works and is perfectly safe.

The General huffs and says, "Those are just numbers. In fact, those are just your numbers.

"I have no idea where they came from or whether the tests were properly conducted or whether the tests were conducted at all.

"All the test subjects from Africa are dead."

My patience is wearing thin and then it hits me!

I shout, "There is only one way you could know the test subjects are all dead Sir!

"What do you know about the attack that wiped out all three African villages and their clinics? What was that, your false flag operation?"

It is then that I realize that none of the cameras are pointing at me. Everyone is removing their headset and putting their mike down.

One of the military men asks, "How much of that went out over the air?"

The Production Manager rewinds the broadcast tape and starts it playing. The monitor shows us talking, and then it ends with, "the test subjects from Africa are dead."

The Production Manager smiles and says, "You must have been aware that we have a seven second delay so we can kill any inappropriate language."

The Production Manager says to the camera, "We apologies for the momentary interruption in our debate.

"Our mobile satellite link was lost, but we're back on now.

"Unfortunately, Professor Gill Bennett has an urgent and pressing engagement and we are all out of time.

"The Surgeon General does wish to make a statement before we conclude this broadcast."

The General says, "I know that people across America want us to conduct studies to determine if the machine is safe for human use. It apparently works on animals. We are not about to subject humans to this kind of experimental medicine at this time.

"Even if we did, it would be a limited test study to determine its effectiveness and whether or not there are any adverse effects. The radiation could pose a public threat is it lingers in the body causing second degree exposure to surrounding people.

"As with other drugs and treatments it can take up to ten years to be approved by the FDA. For these reasons, tests will not be conducted at this time."

The program is concluded and the visitors leave the bunker.

I am depressed.

Nancy reassures me that we will persevere in the end.

I suggest, "Our wedding day is drawing near.

Robert Stetson

"Perhaps we should let there be a clone wedding, just in case.

"It would be their next opportunity to kill us both, Nan".

Nancy bounces up out of her chair and turns to face me, "Getting married is like heart surgery, she says in a firm tone. It doesn't work if you have someone else do it for you.

"The wedding is on and no one had better mess with it.

"Then the day comes. This is our special day."

It turns out to be a very special day, indeed. Nancy looks radiant with all heads turning to look at her with warm smiles.

As for me, well, I'm the groom. I feel like a fifth wheel. People look at me and see a guy whose only job is to make her the bride.

The wedding is all about her, and shouldn't it be?

I am likened to the air in a hot air balloon, the buoyancy in a beautiful yacht, the conductor's baton. I make no sound, nor am I seen, but I propel the performance, for without me, there would be none.

I join the masses and looking adoringly at her.

I've never been so happy. She looks so dainty and frail. I do love her so.

We exchange vows. Her eyes sparkle in the candlelight. Her lips are soft and sweet as she speaks the words. The words are not special, but they sound so tender when spoken in her voice.

My heart is melting.

Then the Priest breaks the spell with his pronouncement and I kiss the bride.

Her taste and aroma intoxicate me. My head is swimming and I just want to be alone with her, forever.

We exit the church and I am so relieved that nothing has happened to ruin our day.

We descend the stairs toward the Limo, which frankly, I'm getting a little tired of riding in. It would be nice to ride in a convertible or at least roll down the windows for a change.

Then shots ring out. They are staging another assassination attempt.

This time it's on the wedding. I bark orders, "This time I expect to see some prisoners. I want to know whose doing this. Got it?"

The Goons yell back, Yes Sir!"

One by one the Goons are falling to the ground doing their silly android dance with a big grin.

I look at Nancy and say, "We have got to fix that damned grinning problem." I'm getting a bit nervous because it doesn't look like we're going to survive this attack.

The Goons are falling fast. The attacking soldiers are moving steadily toward us. It's clear that Nancy and I are the objective of this mission.

Nancy scoops up a machine gun off the ground with one hand and levels the entire front line of attackers in a rage.

She grabs my arm with her other hand and snaps me around bodily toward the Limo.

Her teeth are bared in that famous 'true grit' expression that John Wayne did so well. Gun blazing; she looks for the entire world like an angry commando.

I flop around like a ragdoll in her grip.

My feet never touch the ground as she carries me in her fist through a hail of gunfire on the way to the car.

As she jams me face down onto the floor of the Limo, all you can hear me say is, "Holy Moly!"

You can get away with a lot, but don't ever mess with a lady's wedding.

I don't have to tell you. The honeymoon was a raging success.

Kevin is livid with rage regarding my handling of company business and from what I understand, has taken out a contract on my life.

Any Homicide Detective will tell you that the only thing worse than not having anyone with a motive to kill you, is everyone having a motive to kill you.

Nancy has arranged a meeting of the Board of Directors to present a state of the company report.

I address the Board by opening with, "The only way to return the company to profitability will be to retool the escort androids.

"We have to deprogram them and reprogram them to be used as administrative service androids or factory workers.

"Almost all of the workers at Farmer Industries are being downsized in order to reduce the burden rate over the long hall.

"By restructuring the escort androids to serve as a legitimate labor force, we can put the manufacturing cost of building them to work as an asset.

"To destroy them would create an enormous liability."

The new VP of Finance asks, "You're raising hell with the actuarial tables of every welfare, Social Security and entitlement programs around the world."

I say, "I don't give a damn about Social Security or entitlement programs. That's someone else's problem to solve. I just want to save lives."

The VP of Finance goes on, "If we use android labor and use no human labor, we would be manufacturing billions of dollars in products and services and not generating a penny in taxes.

"We would be paying no wages at all. Won't that bring the federal, state and local governments down on us? ."

I reply with, "Automated warehouses do it all the time. When the rules of the game change, it's time to change the way the game is played.

"All of society is attempting to put a stop to the life extending benefits of the Cure. If we could change the way the Cure effects society, it would be in harmony with the overall acceptance.

"The stopper in his solution stems from the greedy people who have leveraged the status quo to make them-selves rich, powerful, or both.

"Maybe it's time for the basic monetary and reward system to change."

The VP of Manufacturing asks, "To what extent is the escort central processor hardwired for their job?"

The VP of Engineering speaks up with, "We're looking into that. It's likely that hard wiring won't be an issue. It pretty much doesn't matter what task they perform if the retrofits make it possible."

The meeting draws to a close and the room empties out.

Nancy and I are the only two people in the room except for my Goons.

Nancy says, "Your activities overseas have captured the interest of the CIA."

As I gather my notes I say, "Yes, I know. We suspect the attack on our convoy may have been linked to a false flag operation. Now I agree it could very well have been characteristic of CIA activity."

Chapter 6 Betrayal

The grass roots movement is quickly heating up and both the state, local and federal government along with the corporate interests are beginning to be threatened.

The destruction of the clinics in Africa has spawned stories of corruption in high places. The rumors are correct.

In Congress there is debate on the floor.

Congressman Lairing speaks to the current situation, "Some of the fringe groups are demonstrating for the ban of the Cure because it is playing God. Like abortion, it is deemed by some to be immoral. The argument is very similar for both cases. Abortion prevents a soul from entering the world when its time has come.

"Some say it's a sin to force a new baby to be born into an already hopeless situation. In this similar argument, some say the Cure prevents a soul from leaving the world when its time has come.

"Others say the Cure prevents needless suffering and death."

Congressman Eider is resigned to the fact that change is inevitable saying, "I think dramatic changes are coming soon with the Cure being in the mix. Either way we realize that the Cure is going to be forced on us. That will cripple the already burdened Social Security System.

"We have to redesign the monetary system. It will have to be done in a way that doesn't infringe on the status of the wealthy. It also has to be done in a way to maintain the wealthy person's power position, lower the crime rate and enrich the government all at the same time.

Congressman Lairing says, "I agree that a change is needed. Is this the solution?"

Congressman Eider injects, "I agree with any change that will keep the Cure from killing the economy. It's the first step in insulating the special needs of the elderly and the poor from the burden of the government to support them.

"Eliminate hard currency entirely. The process is under way and has been for a very long time. The credit and debit card system is the first step to a cash free society. Wages are paid by direct deposit and purchases are made using the debit card. The bank transfers the electronic currency to the vendor, whose bank pays the wholesaler by electronic transfer. Everyone involved pays bills using automatic bill payer. No one ever sees hard currency.

"Violent robberies are eliminated because there is no cash to steal.

"The means are already at our disposal."

Congressman Bowling was once a former technologist and understands the problem of exponentially accelerating change.

He stands and speaks, "The people are driving change that we're not ready to implement, but the time to implement is now. To begin with we have already made changes in the banking currency system. We need only announce the change in currency right now.

"Let's focus on meeting the larger problem of financial dynamics.

Congressman Lairing enumerates the features with, "Here's how we're going to sell the change to the people. Tell them the benefits of digital currency, such as no theft, no embezzlement, no violent robberies, and no lost paper money. Every dime is securely at their disposal. Your money is more secure.

"No need for making change at the point of sale. Checkout counters don't handle the actual money. Employee theft is minimized. Lines move more swiftly. The public is enriched in many ways. I think people will be demanding digital currency after we place all the advertising to promote the idea.

Congressman Lairing enumerates the benefits with, "What this means to us is that the underground economy of flea markets and personal sales are eliminated.

"Our statistics show that we lose trillions of dollars in lost taxes because people exchange products and services for cash without reporting the income or the sales tax. We will now be monitoring the bank transfers on every exchange.

Congressman Lairing now gives us the bottom line with, "What this truly means to us is that the resulting revenues from 100% sales reporting will generate more cash flow into our tax base than the increase in payments out to Social Security. We will benefit from the implementation of the new currency model even though we lose the war on the Cure.

Congressman Bowling says, "Good plan. Let's go with it. In the meantime I think we should continue to stall or eliminate the Cure as an impetus to our revenues. Why settle for a financial win when we can have a total victory? We need to take another shot at shutting down Farmer Industries. I'm in touch with the boys who can do it."

Congress contacts the Board of Health and the AMA's Legal Teams. The Board of Health demands to inspect the Farmer Industries building for adherence to standards required of the health care manufacturing industry.

The American Medical Association is investigating the use of hardware to cure disease as a violation of the requirement to obtain a license to practice medicine.

All evidence up to now indicates that the Cure has been administered by licensed Veterinarians and any human testing by licensed medical personnel, but a court challenge to that effect would slow things down.

Also, the legal teams are looking into whether or not the machine used in the Cure should have the proper AMA certifications for use as medical equipment. The machine could be viewed as a peace of invasive surgical equipment.

While the government is plotting to either eliminate the threat imposed by The Cure, the underworld is plotting to destroy the President of Farmer Industries in a bid for revenge.

Over at the headquarters of the crime syndicate, Joe the Bull is holding a Mafia meeting to discuss the best way to deal with Farmer Industries and the shutting down of the many Prostitution centers around the world.

Joe pounds the table and says, "We had a profitable, legal way to clean up. We were making a killing here and then Gill Bennett steps in and shuts us down. There are no laws yet governing the use of the android ladies used in our pleasure clubs. We are untouchable."

A guy nicknamed Stomper chimes in, "If we can eliminate Gill Bennett we can get the factories turned on again, but we have to get him where he lives, at Farmer Industries."

Joe the Bull says, "You're out of your mind! Farmer Industries has an army of Goons to protect this guy. How are we going to get past them?"

Stomper chuckles then rolls out a blackboard with a diagram on it.

He points to the layout of the factory complex and says, "We pull together a fleet of twelve armored trucks and paint them up to look like Farmer Industries Security.

"Then we wheel in through the back gate after we cut the lock and when we're on top of them, we let loose with our guns, ammo and heavy artillery.

"We blast our way in and snuff out Gill Bennett.

"His android Goons won't know what to do. They will think we're them."

Joe nods and says, "Wow! That's a plan. How soon can we get this damn thing going?"

Stomper smiles and says, "The boys and I have already put it together. We have the twelve trucks, artillery and uniforms in place. I have seventy men ready to kick butt.

"We are planning this for 12 Noon on the first of August. It's a Monday, so things should be humming and Gill will be sure and be there."

The health and insurance industry are busy putting a plan together to save their businesses from the scourge called The Cure.

If The Cure is legalized for humans, it will mean the end of profitability for them all.

A band of renegade soldiers of fortune are meeting in a desert complex just west of the city.

Colonel Harding is holding a muster to discuss the best way to deal with

Farmer Industries and the shutting down of the many Cure centers around the world.

He pounds the table and says, "Farmer Industries is about to destroy the health care, insurance and the pharmaceutical industries with that damned machine. Gill Bennett is the cause of the problem and we need to take him out.

"We've been commissioned to take out Farmer Industries in general and Gill Bennett in particular."

The Colonel rolls out a blackboard with what looks like a scrimmage plan for a football game.

He points to the board and says, "We will pull together a fleet of fourteen armored trucks and paint them up to look like Farmer Industries Security.

"Then we wheel in through the side gate after we cut the lock and when we're on top of them, we let loose with our guns, ammo and heavy artillery. We blast our way in and snuff out Gill Bennett.

"His android Goons won't know what to do. They will think we're them.

General Dismay says, "Wow! That's a plan. How soon can we get this damn thing going?"

The Colonel smiles and says, "The boys and I have already put it together. We have the fourteen trucks, artillery and uniforms in place. I have eighty men ready to kick butt.

"We are planning this for 12 Noon on the first of August. It's a Monday, so things should be humming and Gill will be sure and be there."

Kevin Farmer, My former partner is plotting a little revenge of his own. He wants me dead and has put a plan together.

Kevin Farmer is on the phone with Moose from his old gang and says, "Gill Bennett is the cause of all our problems and we need to take him out.

"We've already pulled together a fleet of ten armored trucks and paint them up to look like Farmer Industries Security. We plan to wheel right in through the front gate without stopping for the guard house and after we're on top of them, we let loose with our guns, ammo and heavy artillery.

"We blast our way in and snuff out Gill Bennett. Once we're inside his android Goons won't know what to do. They will think we're them.

Moose says, "Wow! That's a plan. How soon can we get this damn thing going?"

Kevin smiles and says, "The boys and I have already put it together. We have the ten trucks, artillery and uniforms in place. I have sixty five men ready to kick butt.

"We are planning this for 12 Noon on the first of August. It's a Monday, so things should be humming and Gill will be sure and be there."

It's August first at 12 Noon. It's a quiet Monday with sunshine and a soft balmy breeze. The android factory is humming along in full production mode. Androids need no breaks or lunch.

Gill Bennett is in his bunker office with the VPs of Marketing, Finance and Manufacturing.

Vice President of World Markets, Dr. Martin Gold is visiting and is interested in knowing more about the future of our android line for use in security.

He has had many requests from countries in and around some of the political hot spots.

The conversation is light and we are settling in to enjoy a quiet lunch bring provided by our small android kitchen staff.

At the back gate there are seventy Mafia Soldiers in Farmer Industry Goon suits and twelve armored vehicles with Farmer Industry logos on the side.

There is a pinging sound as the bolt cutters snap the lock.

Off in the distance there is another pinging sound as the bolt cutters pop the lock on the side gate and eighty Soldiers of Fortune hired by the healthcare industry in Goon suits with fourteen armored trucks with Farmer Industry logos begin their entry into the complex.

There is some confusion in the camera room where the area clearly shows a full complement of one hundred and fifty total Goons and twenty six armored vehicles.

All the control room Goons move their heads in a little closer to the monitors to get a better look at the area where the alarm shows there is an intrusion.

The area not only looks free of intruders, but is well fortified with their security teams. All the control room Goons settle back into their seats and watch the area a little more closely.

Meanwhile, up at the front gate, Kevin Farmer's henchmen have lined up the ten armored trucks and sixty five men. They move swiftly toward the front gate where they blast their way through and continue in the direction of the complex center.

It's then that each of the three invading armies sees the other two coming at them.

They each marvel at the size and speed of the apparent Farmer Industries response and open fire. There are now thirty six armored vehicles and two hundred phony Goons converging on the complex center.

Gill, Martin and all the other VPs jump to their feet as the warning alarms blast.

The wall-to-wall video screens flicker to life in the bunker with a full sized view of the live action going on above them on the surface.

The seventy man army and the eighty man army and the sixty five man army are all slugging it out.

I get on the intercom to the control room and say, "Hold your position. I don't want any of you to respond to the battle just yet. Hold back and let it play out."

"What the hell is happening up there?" martin exclaims.

I just smile and say, "Looks like three armies have all decided to attack today at noon. What are the odds? And to beat it all, it looks like they all camouflaged themselves to look like our soldiers to confuse us."

The VP of Security says, "Let's have a seat and watch the show."

He turns to the android waiter and says, "How about some popcorn and a cola beverage? How about you guys?" We all sink into our seats and enjoy some refreshments while we watch the show.

I say, "Yes, our security teams can finish off what's left of the winners."

In the sky overhead a Police Helicopter appears and looks down on the skirmish with amazement.

"Looks like Gill's Goons have all gone loony tunes" the pilot reports over the radio.

I don't see anything but Goons slaughtering each other. It's a madhouse down there.

On the ground the three armies are phoning or radioing back to their units to report that they are severely outnumbered and need to retreat.

As they begin to back out of the complex the way they came in, the Police Helicopter pilot reports, "The Goons have gone completely crazy! They're killing everything they see!"

Then the call goes out that the three armies of Killer Goons are leaving the compound and heading for the town by different paths.

Over the Police radio a voice cries out, "Get the National Guard and all available units in here. If these things get to the town it will be a bloodbath."

Within minutes fighter planes come streaking through followed by Blackhawk Helicopters.

All three of the Goon armies are engaged in battle with the National Guard and the local Police. All troops of the phony invading Goon armies are either captured or destroyed.

Meanwhile, back at Farmer Industries, Martin asks, "Gill, how did you know so quickly that these weren't your Goons and vehicles?"

I just wave my hand at the screen and say, "Hell, I don't have a couple of hundred Goons and all those trucks out there in the first place. In the second place, what with all the alarms going off, where were the intruders? It's obvious that there is something weird going on out there."

Martin shakes his head and says, "It was pretty much all over before I realized what was happening."

I ease back in my seat and say, "Another clue was all the blood and gore out there. Goons would have been a cleaner kill. What a mess."

Now I can't give the go ahead for the Goons to clean up the mess or reestablish the gate area. It will have to remain as it is until the Police investigators give the go ahead to clean up.

I have the Goons do a temporary makeshift security checkpoint at the front gate.

I call the Police and report the attack, but that wasn't really necessary because the helicopter reported it while it was in progress.

I'm dreading the visit from the Police knowing the odds are good Lieutenant Daggett will be among them.

A call comes in from the lobby. It's a lady android who says, "Sir, the Police are here with the coroner and a fleet of ambulances and four hearses."

I respond immediately, "Yes, I'll be right up."

My team of VPs and I gather our things and head for the elevator.

When the elevator doors open, there stands Lieutenant Daggett.

I extend my hand in a gesture of friendliness and greet him, "Hello Lieutenant. Good to see you're on the case."

He responds by reaching out for my hand.

Before I realize his hand isn't empty, I feel the metal on my wrist and I am wearing a handcuff on my right wrist. He spins me around and presses me against the wall, artfully bringing my left hand around behind me to join the other handcuff and complete the capture.

I hear his voice behind me say, "Yes, Professor. Good to see you too." He reads me my rights and sits me down. "You are under arrest for the multiple murders of the people here at your facility."

He turns to the VP's and says, "None of you are under arrest, but we are detaining you for questioning. Let's all go downtown.

A group of Police Officers close in and handcuff the VP's taking each of us to a separate car so we can't have a conversation with one another before questioning.

When we arrive at the Police Station I am ushered into a small room and left sitting alone for about twenty minutes. It is clearly a ploy to soften me up before questioning. I am supposed to fret about the situation and heighten my anticipation. I am not impressed.

When Lieutenant Daggett enters the room with another Detective and two uniformed Officers I demand, "I want to see Attorney Car. I want him present before and during any questioning.

Lieutenant Daggett pounds the table and shouts, "You can try to weasel your way out of this, but your buddies have already sold you out!"

The other Detective says to Lieutenant Daggett, "Calm down, Bill. This guy looks pretty reasonable to me. I'm sure we can work with him."

Then he introduces himself, "I'm Lieutenant Detective Hall. You want to do the right thing, I'm sure. We can work with you and, believe it or not, we are actually on your side. I'm sure there is a reasonable explanation for all of this. You can help us to help you by telling us what we need to know, or we can wait for your Attorney to get here and wring it out of you. What would you like to do?"

Now I'm insulted.

I look the Detective in the eye and shout, "Cut the good cop bad cop crap! Get my lawyer in here!"

Robert Stetson

They both leave without speaking.

Things take a turn for the better when Car makes an appearance.

He insists on a change of room and says, "I want a room with no mirrors and no cameras so my client can speak freely. What's going on behind that wall to wall mirror over there?"

The Detective suggests, "All of the rooms in this place have either wall to wall mirrors or black bubbles in the ceiling containing cameras.

You can meet at the corner table in the cafeteria."

As we're sitting in the corner of the cafeteria I say, "Lieutenant Daggett told me the VPs all sold me out. What the hell is he talking about?"

Car smiles and says, "I was present at the questioning of all of them. Your staff of VPs definitely has no idea what the massacre was all about. They only know that the Goons in the conflict were humans, not androids."

"So! Daggett is lying through his teeth!" I sneered.

Attorney Car smiles again and says, "What's new?

The Police will tell you anything to get you to confess if you're guilty, or turn the goods on your buddies to save yourself. It's what they do. He told each of them that you sold them out. The courts have maintained that the Police are allowed to lie in order to obtain information from a captive."

Now I really get angry.

Attorney Car asks, "What the hell happened out there, Gill? It isn't so much that they all tried to kill each other; it's that they turned and started to move on the whole town. The Police naturally conclude that the hordes of crazies were going to town in order to continue the rampage. Why would over a hundred men commit suicide just to make it look like your Goons went nuts?"

I say, "It's a puzzle and I can't imagine what was happening out there."

Car says, "The Police have taken a few prisoners from those who survived the battle, but the Police aren't telling anything they discover until they conclude their investigation."

I shake my head in disbelief and ask, "Am I being formally charged with anything?"

Car looks down at the table and says, "Not yet, but Daggett has his eye on murder one. He's hoping to crack this case and shut down Farmer Industries in the process.

"We have to find out why he's so preoccupied with eliminating Farmer Industries. It occurs to me that he might be on the take from someone."

Lieutenant Daggett saunters up to the table and says, "You're free to go, Professor Bennett. Sorry for the inconvenience."

"Why are you releasing me so soon?" I ask.

He just says, "We have nine survivors from apparently three different groups. You're a popular guy, Gill. I'd be watching my back if I were you."

Attorney Car speaks up, "If my client's life is in danger you have an obligation to tell him who is posing the threat. Just who were these people?"

The Lieutenant grunts and says, "The mob, Industry sources, and some soldiers of fortune."

I say, "Soldiers of fortune?"

He says, "We don't know who hired them and neither do they, but they are mercenaries."

Attorney Car, the VPs and I all meet back at the bunker.

Meanwhile, back at mob headquarters Joe the Bull puffs vigorously on his cigar moaning, "Where did Bennett get all those troops and trucks? What happened over there?

"I'm glad we used stolen vehicles. Hank at the chop shop did a great job on the paint job. We lost the whole fleet of trucks.

"We had better lay low a while."

The mob platoon has four men who are in Police captivity at the hospital and they are doing well. The Police have scheduled all four for interrogation the following day as soon as they are well enough to be questioned.

Colonel Harding is one of the two survivors captured by the Police from the health care industry platoon and is being held in a hospital complex under guard. So far Colonel Harding hasn't given the people in the health care industry away to the Police but is scheduled for interrogation the following day as soon as they are well enough to be questioned. These two men are both injured rather badly, but not critically. They are essentially under the care of the health care industry people who hired them.

The next morning they are both dead from an embolism. The deaths were unfortunate and unexpected.

As a formality, the Police had an investigation into the deaths headed up by Lieutenant Daggett. The deaths were ruled as being from natural causes.

At the penitentiary, Kevin Farmer is just getting the news that his henchmen are either dead or in Police custody. Kevin is distraught because he knows he can get the death penalty if the wrong people are in custody and talk. They know too much and can easily cut a deal.

Kevin calls Lieutenant Daggett in a panic and blurts out, "Who do you have in custody? I need these people eliminated before they can point any fingers!"

Lieutenant Daggett says, "Damn you Kevin! I told you; never call me on this phone. I also told you I'd take care of it. Hang up!"

Kevin says, "You had better get over here right away. Al Akken is in a panic and says we're not taking the fall for this. I need to talk to you."

Lieutenant Daggett's interrogation focuses heavily on the four survivors from the mob platoon. They ultimately gave up the name, "Joe the Bull" as being the one who orchestrated the attack. The Police report reveals that the mob set this whole thing up and Joe the Bull is indicted for over one hundred counts of murder.

On the news, the financial picture around the world is changing as the citizens of all countries are required to have ID Cards that double as a financial transfer control medium.

The news anchor says, "All cash in all country denominations will be invalid in thirty days. Gather up your money folks and head to the bank. Empty your cookie jars and piggy banks. Every coin and paperback will become trash in 30 days."

The co-anchor speaks, "In other news, there will be a mass mailing of ID Cards to every legal citizen of every country on Earth.

"The sixteen digit number of your ID card will be your key to financial survival from this day on. Cards may be obtained by either waiting for your card to come in the mail, or at your local bank of choice.

"The first five digits will be your bank identification number, the sixth number will be your financial status a zero being Social Security recipient through nine which denotes a billionaire, the seventh being your occupational status whether employed, unemployed or self-employed. The rest of the digits include your country code and personal ID number.

"Your number will change as you move through life according to your financial and work status."

The anchor chimes in with, "A thirty percent tax by each country will be imposed on the spot for all cash deposits.

"Your chosen bank will monitor and regulate the changes in status and reissue cards as required."

The co-anchor looks over at the anchor and asks, "What do you think of that, Jane?"

The anchor says "Ouch!

"If you're not a citizen of the country that you currently reside in, call the Immigration Department for instructions.

"If you receive Social Security checks by mail, call the Social Security Office for instructions on how to have your payments direct deposited to your bank account.

"If you receive unemployment compensation by check call your Employment Office.

"If you're receiving any annuity or other income by check, call the agency responsible for your income."

The co-anchor closes with, "If you don't have a bank account, you had better get one right away or you will be unable to make any purchases in the future.

People are protesting in the streets while the government is busy selling the new electronics only currency.   The selling points are;

1.Drug deals are documented as to the buyers and sellers. People who continuously receive electronic transfers from around the area where they live are contacted about their apparent business activities in the absence of a business license.

2.No one can rob anyone if there is no cash to hand over. Shops and individuals will only have their transfer card on them, not cash. If they are forced to put their thumb print on the transfer, the identity of the robber will be recorded as the receiver of the electronic transfer.

3.Identity theft would be eliminated because the use of a bogus loan thumb print wouldn't match the true owner of the account to be associated with payment. The thumb print of the ID thief would be on the illegal loan document giving away the identity of the felon.

4.Illegal immigrants would be identified when they attempt to open a bank account without having a valid and verified birth certificate and valid Social Security number on file with the State and Federal Government.

5.Fugitives from the law would find it impossible to hide when they have to make purchases. Their account could be flagged as belonging to a fugitive and automatic reporting software would alert the authorities of their geographical whereabouts.

6.Forgery would be eliminated because the thumb print of the forger would be on the illegal document giving away the identity of the felon.

7.Counterfeiting would be eliminated because the banks track every credit by serial number. There is no document to print as hard currency does not exist.

8.Illegal activities such as drugs, prostitution, gambling and graft are flagged and taxed.

9.Embezzlement becomes impossible because the transfer would be recorded and reported to the company as it happens.

The list goes on and on.

The people object to the new monetary system because;

1.It's perceived as an invasion of privacy. The government tracks every dime along with every transaction.
2.Flea market sales would be tracked as income.
3.Private sales between people, no matter how small, would be visible and taxable.
4.Forces licensing of businesses otherwise conducted secretly.
5.Tips become fair game for taxation.
6.Even children's allowances become fair game for taxation.
The anger of the public creates a split between two factions and while the people are fighting between themselves, the government quietly enforces the change.

Pro-cash demonstrations are springing up around the world while the anti-cash demonstrations also appear causing riots in the street.

No one is able to mount a campaign to stop the government because amid the chaos, no one can organize.

The confusion of the public over money is so great that they have lost sight of The Cure.

We, the staff of Farmer Industries are meeting to see if we can find a way to reawaken the furor over The Cure and the public's right to extend the lives of the terminally ill.

Martin suggests, "What if we advertise on the side of busses, television, radio and billboards?"

Nancy injects an idea, "We can start a magazine and call it, "The Cure." The Cure magazine will feature cute animals on the cover. It will capture the interest of all animal lovers and give us a platform for articles and editorials.

"We can feature medical opinions that cause speculation as to whether or not the Cure will be safe for humans.

"We can publish an expose on the African study, how it was conducted and how the village and clinics were attacked by mercenaries."

Attorney Car says, "We can leverage on the concept of the free press and the first amendment rights of the publisher.

"We will price the magazine at one hundred credits, which equates to a dollar. It will be the cheapest and most powerful advertising we can ever buy."

We all bought into this as a good start on the road to public awareness.

Car further informs us, "The Secret Service has advised me that the 3D chipset is released for distribution to the world as long as we don't release the manufacturing and design information.

"Furthermore, any 3D chipset sold must not have the ability to function as a weapon. We must also furnish each 3D chip a serial number that will be satellite linked to our database and be capable of being deactivated by our security center. Since each 3D chip is already satellite linked by satellite to an atomic clock, transmitting the serial number is easy."

In view of the release on the sale of androids and Cure machines, we are bringing a Director of Sales on board from the medical electronics industry to build a sales team.

I have contacted the news media regarding the tour we talked about during their prior visit. We can not only allow a tour of the Cure Factory, but we can now include the Android Factory as well.

The 3D Chip Factory will still be off limits.

I get Amy Kravis on the phone and ask, "Amy, any chance you can come for that tour we talked about?" .

Amy says, "Yes. We would love to see your factory and warehouse, but I will have to clear it with my Production Manager."

I say, "Let him know we can include the android manufacturing line. We are offering them for sale now to the general public."

Amy asks, "What would the androids be used for?"

I let her know, "They would be used in everything from domestic help to factory and clerical work. They are extremely versatile and with the advent of our new chipset, they now rival the intelligence of the average person. After your exclusive tour, we will be having a press conference."

Amy says, "I'll get back to you on the tour. Let me just pencil it in. I'm pretty sure the Producer will give me the O.K."

Amy calls and confirms the tour time and date.

We get the general news media alerted to a news conference.

We don't publicize that Amy will be getting a private tour as that would create a lot of phone calls and inquiries.

Amy arrives with her camera crew and we begin with a short presentation regarding both the Cure and android manufacturing.

I tell her, "The Cure was originally three machines connected by cables and used in sequence to determine the cause of the illness and whether or not the treatment would be effective.

"If the treatment proved to be of a type that can't be cured by the machine, the process would stop there.

"Now we have integrated our 3D chipset into a single intelligent machine that automates the process. We can't show you or talk about the 3D chipset that forms the foundation of all our intelligent products."

We board an electric cart driven by an android and move smoothly through a set of double doors and travel the length of a long tunnel.

Amy seems unaware that the driver isn't a human and asks him, "How long have you been with Farmer Industries?"

The android smiles and says, "I was manufactured on July eleventh of this year.

I am a personal service android with the latest programming for housekeeping and factory transportation. My programs are the highest revision level."

I was surprised by the personal pride he displayed.

Our cart glides through another set of double doors and onto the main isle of the Cure factory floor. The rows of chambers went on for a hundred yards in all directions.

I tell Amy, "We have a six month backlog of orders from veterinarians all over the world. We also have hundreds of new confidential orders that we are not allowed to disclose. Our customer list is a closely guarded secret."

The room is full of factory workers doing a variety of assembly tasks.

"An electric card passes us moving swiftly down the corridor and then takes a sharp turn to the right. It is obviously a parts delivery as the cart is occupied only by a platform stacked high with plain white boxes about one foot square. The boxes would fly from the platform were it not for the Plexiglas side panels holding them in place.

Nancy points at the cart and says, "Our parts delivery is completely automated. That cart is from the 3D chipset factory.

"Each Cure unit gets one of those. The 3D chips are the brains of the Cure and are preprogrammed and tested."

I inject, "We aren't allowed to disclose the manufacturing process, so we won't be visiting that facility today."

Amy looks wide-eyed at the size of the room and the number of workers and Cure machines. She asks, "How many employees do you have here?"

I turn to her and say, "Nancy and I are the only humans you will see today while we are in the factories, except for your team of course. Our Senior Staff and Engineering Department are the only two departments in this entire complex with employees."

Our cart continues on until it comes to another set of double doors. The cart passes through the doors and makes a sharp left-hand turn. We travel for about two hundred yards and pass through another set of double doors into a factory floor with hundreds of bodies hanging down by hooks from an overhead conveyer.

The scene would be gruesome if it weren't for the obvious fact that these are androids in the process of assembly. The bodies are grey and the heads are open and empty from the eyes up. Inside the skulls you can see a variety of sockets waiting for their components to be plugged in.

I point to the parade of suspended bodies and say, "Notice that no two of the faces look alike. We dynamically mold the faces under computer control with a careful eye toward making each androids face look different. We found out early on how hard it is to make each face unique.

"Some of our special order androids have faces made to order. People actually send in head and face plaster molds of the person the android is supposed to resemble."

A parts delivery cart speeds by with a platform loaded with legs. Another cart speeds by with one foot cubic boxes.

Amy looks at me with an inquisitive glance.

I say, "Yes, those are the 3D Chipsets for the brain."

Each android has a toe tag that identifies the unit parameters and the buyer identification.

I say to the driver, "Stop at the 3D Chipset installation station."

The driver nods and says, "Yes, sir."

When we arrive at the 3D Chipset installation station, the workers are opening the boxes and carefully seating the 3D Chipset brain into the skull and clamping it in place. The unit is activated and the android stands up.

It looks off into space for a full minute and announces, "All systems normal."

The androids walk several feet and are picked up by a sling that carries them horizontally through a hole in the wall about ten feet off the floor.

I smile and say, "These androids are on their way to our next stop."

Our cart lurches forward and picks up speed. It continues to the opposite end of the room and, once again, goes through a set of double doors turning right as it enters to corridor. In a few feet the cart makes another right turn through double doors and into a room with a strange smell.

"Amy, I apologize for the odor, but this is what we call the skin room."

Overhead, the sling that holds the android horizontal stops and then lowers the body into a vat. Some of the vats are finishing their process and the android is lifted out.

I tell Amy, "The next stop is the finishing station where the eyelids are cut and eyebrows and eyelashes are put in place. These small details have to be done by hand. The hand that does them belongs to a specially programmed android.

"Hair is surgically implanted in the head or on the face to form beards and mustaches. When the finishing touches are completed each android walks to the distribution center near the front of the factory complex and sit in a waiting room after checking in with the front desk."

The cart moves on and takes us to the waiting room.

I say, "There are one thousand chairs in the room and only about eighty are occupied at the moment."

A bus pulls up and the androids all rise and board the bus without being told.

I smile and say, "This concludes our tour. The bus will take the finished product to the distribution center where they will be sent to their final delivery point, some by rail, some by local vans, and some by chartered airplanes."

Amy asks, "How much do they sell for?"

I say, "From 100,000,000 credits (about $1M) to 200,000,000 credits (about $2M) depending on the model number, special physical attributes and any special programming options, plus delivery charge."

When we arrive back at the bunker, Harvey, our android chef has a hot soup and sandwich lunch waiting. The press conference is scheduled for 2:00 PM.

We have time to relax and talk about the past trials and tribulations with regard to the Cure.

I explain, "The android manufacturing and sales raises money for out primary program. It's all been about The Cure. My only goal is to provide life-giving aid to the terminally ill.

The process of developing, manufacturing and delivering the product has met with resistance by dozens of groups and individuals who stand to lose financially from the Cure. You would think people would value the lives of their dying neighbors over a few dollars."

Amy says, "Who are these people?"

I responded, "These are Healthcare groups, Insurance groups, government groups and people who have a personal interest. The groups are the worst because as a member of a group, no one is taking personal responsibility for the things they do."

Amy is writing in her notebook.

An android service worker walks over and says, "The media is here, sir. They are waiting in the conference room and it's time to begin the press conference."

The press conference begins and I share everything I told Amy and added a few interesting examples of the product features.

Then it comes time to talk about the organized interference with product testing I share the film footage where the African boy is cured of terminal cancer, the attack on the village and clinic, and the interview with the Surgeon General aired by the TV news media at the time.

The reporters are writing frantically and are pointing their cameras at the viewing screen during the showing.

I say, "No need to try and capture any of the video portions of this conference. I have copies of the videos to take with you."

I am asked, "What information do you have regarding this new magazine called "The Cure"?"

I say, "I have taken the liberty of enclosing ten free copies of this month's issue of The Cure in your press kits. Hope you enjoy it and mention it in your news reports."

The conference wraps up and we have an open bar with a full party compliment of horderves and snacks.

As Nancy and I leave the room, I say, "Enjoy the refreshments. Stay as long as you like. I there is anything you need, just ask one of the wait staff.

The next day there are numerous television expose's presenting the facts regarding The Cure machine and its proven potential for good. Newspapers and magazines are filled with the photos and editorials based on the news conference.

The next morning there are crowds with picket signs blocking the city Halls and town halls, insurance companies, hospitals and clinics along with government buildings.

There are riots in the streets and general civil unrest erupts everywhere. Medical University riots spill out into the streets and the National Guard and State Police are called in to restore the peace, but as usual, the Police escalate the violence with clubs and mace.

The third day brings a realization that instead of moving us in the direction of product acceptance, we are shut down.

The process server just left us a summons demanding that we immediately cease and desist all manufacturing and sales of The Cure for any purposes with the exception of those ordered by the United States federal and state government offices. The product has had an injunction placed on it until further notice.

The news media picks up the story and reports that pet owners will no longer be able to have their pets treated for terminal illnesses.

A government spokesperson says, "We have determined that the curing of these terminal diseases have caused undesired results in the years past treatment. One example was a Great Dane named Howard who was treated for cancer and died of heart failure only two years later due to cardiac complications caused by The Cure."

I recoiled in horror and say, "Harvey only had three months left to live. He was ten years old when we treated him! We gave Harvey two more years of life."

Nancy says, "Harvey was one of my favorites. He already had a heart problem when we admitted him for treatment!"

In The Cure magazine for the following month, we include the complete transcript from the government spokesperson's talk on the news the month before along with the true story of Harvey the dog.

As is always true of the general public, their memory is short and their attention span is nonexistent.

The articles have no real effect on the perception of the public. They take the two accounts separately, not realizing they are being duped.

On the brighter side, the pro-Cure demonstrations continue.

The injunction on our product manufacture and sales continues as well pending a court hearing to determine the merit of the injunction.

A letter comes from the court scheduling the hearing for the end of next year.

I reach for the phone to call Car about getting the court hearing moved up, but it rings before I can pick it up.

I answer it with, "Hello?"

Car Bentley of the Bentley & Bentley Law Firm is on the line saying, "Gill! Glad I caught you in. We've got a problem."

"Yes, I just opened the mail, Car. What are we going to do?"

Car says, "I'm working on it. If the injunction continues you will be out of business in six months tops."

Meanwhile, I'm busy stopping production on the 3D Chipsets and other critical components for the Cure production lines and writing letters to the customers who have orders pending.

The reaction from around the world is swift and extreme.

With thirty five percent of our orders coming from countries having diplomatic ties and the units being destined for the clinics that support the needs of their royalty, there is a hewn cry in diplomatic circles.

Washington is under siege and the justice system is under siege from

Robert Stetson

Washington.

The federal court clerk who was told to push the hearing out as far as possible is fired and replaced to protect the bureaucrat who gave him the order to delay the hearing.

Our hearing is rescheduled for next month to allow us time to prepare.

In the meantime our production capacity has been diverted to filling the various backorders for the androids. We're making up about 50% of the lost revenue by increasing the filling of backorders of the only product we have left to market, the android.

Our hearing date arrives and the courtroom is filled to capacity with dignitaries from around the world.

Most noticeable are the sheiks in their white garb and ornate headbands. There are armies of various security personnel standing around the perimeter of the room to each guard their royal master.

The judge is visibly intimidated.

The U.S. President has called the court and has ordered the hearing to be put on hold.

All news people are told they have to leave the building.

As the Secret Service enters the room forming a corridor of men down both sides of the isle, the President walks down the middle and relieves the judge of his post saying, "I will conduct this hearing today."

He looks over at me and says, "I understand there is an embargo on all your outgoing shipments and an injunction of your product manufacture stemming from the lack of license required to manufacture invasive healthcare products, is that right?"

I stand and say, "That's correct sir."

The President speaks again, "I hereby proclaim all injunctions and embargos lifted and all legal actions pending to be dropped immediately by executive order of the President of the United States."

I ask, "While we have you here, sir is it possible to proclaim that The Cure is safe for use on humans?"

The President lets out a laugh and winks at me saying, "Don't press your luck. I'm not touching that one."

Production is restarted on the Cure machines and the custom 3D Chips used in the product.

New letters go out letting everyone know that the embargo is lifted and the units will be shipped as soon as we can get them through manufacturing and testing.

A full article is published in The Cure magazine giving a complete rendition of the hearing.

The resulting outcome of the embargo lifting and restrictions on the use of the machine to cure animals until a hearing could be conducted has a positive and a negative effect on Farmer Industries future. The positive outcome is the restarting of full production on the backordered units.

New orders start coming in at twice the rate that they were. The negative effect is that almost half of the animal rights people declared victory, had parties and went home. They stopped their protest marches.

Robert Stetson

Chapter 7 Hard Labor

Nancy and I are tired from all the aggravation that's been plaguing us. I just want to whisk her away on a second honeymoon in Rome.

I want it to be a surprise, so I have our travel office arrange the trip. Our company jumbo jet will have to be prepped for the trip and winter is setting in. I have our trip scheduled for late spring so she can enjoy the flowers and sidewalk cafes.

Nancy being Nancy, she is on top of everything that goes on. She is more than an administrative assistant, she is my business partner.

We are enjoying dinner she is telling me how much she loves me as she does every day. She says, "I can't tell you how much I'm looking forward to our trip to Rome in the late spring."

I am amazed at her knowing about the trip. I ask her, "How did you find out? I just arranged it this afternoon and said not to tell anyone."

She looks back at me and says, "I was looking over the maintenance logs for the airplanes and saw a maintenance work order to prep for a flight to Rome for both of us."

I just shake my head and say, "You don't miss a thing do you honey?"

She just smiles back at me and winks.

My heart melts. I love her so much.

Some of our androids are different than they used to be, but I can't quite put a handle on it. I notice that on the one hand you can't tell any of them anything without all of them being aware of what you said. If you tell one of them anything different than you told the last one, they get confused. On the other hand, if you train one of them to do something, the others are suddenly able to do it as well. It's as though they share a common consciousness.

I tell my engineering staff to look into what is going on here.

Our sales staff receives a call from the Ramos Clinic in Columbia South America ordering three hundred of the Goon model androids. They also order three Cure machines for their central clinic in Tunja located nearby in the Andes Mountains. They have the credits (cash) waiting in a Manhattan bank for the transaction. They invite Nancy and me to bring a staff of researchers to work with them and assist them in establishing the safety of The Cure for use on humans.

I am excited at the prospect. It's a golden opportunity. Nancy and I pack our bags and leave for Villavicencio, Columbia on our Lear Jet.

The airstrip there is only about fifteen miles from Bogotá and the roads are good. Columbia is peppered with small airport runways because the Andes make travel problematic. It seems as though almost everyone there has a light aircraft for transportation.

As our Lear Jet touches down in Villavicencio, we are met by a big black shiny limousine and a man with a broad grin. He wears a straw hat and has clothing made of some material resembling burlap.

He says, "Welcome to Columbia my friends. My name is Carlos and I will be your guide and your servant while you visit here."

Nancy and I smile back and shake his leathery hand.

His face is brown and rugged. Carlos' Looks for the entire world like the man in the coffee bean commercial right down to his sandals.

The ride to their company headquarters is pleasant. Their company limo has a full bar, a satellite TV and the current newspapers. Who knew you could find the Wall Street Journal here in South America.

In about twenty five minutes we arrive at the entrance to Bogotá Health Industries, LLC.

As we are escorted into the Ramos Clinic building I am amazed at the beauty of the facility which is composed of mirrored panes of glass in its entirety.

Once inside there are no outer walls, only floor to ceiling, wall to wall window to the outside world. The view is spectacular. I never imagined that Columbia was such a beautiful place or that their medical facilities are so advanced.

The floors and inner walls are polished marble.

We are led onto an elevator and go to the top floor. When the doors open we are in an office.

This office must be a full acre because it's the only room on this floor. The desk is huge and the man behind it looks small by comparison.

The man rises and walks slowly toward Nancy and me with his hand outstretched.

He says, "My name is Miguel. I am the President of this fine institution we call Ramos Clinic. Did you have a pleasant journey?"

I shake his hand and say, "Very pleasant trip. We're glad to be here." After seeing his apparently small stature behind that huge desk it is surprising to see that Miguel is actually about six foot two inches tall.

Miguel says, "In much the way you have selected the location for your Swiss factories, we have decided to locate our clinic in Tunja. It's located at the base of a cliff wall in an elevated location to make it strategically easier to defend against attack.

"Also, the location eliminates risk to surrounding villages."

I ask, "Doesn't this make treatment difficult for the poorer people in your population? They may not be able to travel as freely as the wealthier among you."

Miguel says, "We will be providing free transportation originating from a central location in downtown Bogota. People will be transported to The Cure center in Tunja where they are housed in a barracks environment until they can be treated.

'Then we have recovery areas where they can stay until the toxins are successfully eliminated."

I ask Miguel, "Three hundred Goon model androids is a lot. Are all of these destined for Tunja?"

Miguel answers, "Most of them are, but I have reserved a few for protection services to be used in my offices, much as you have."

I make a comment, "I suggest you have armored vehicles and use AK47s and Israel Arms Desert Eagle .440 caliber side arms."

Miguel says, "We have a budget for this and these things are on the list. The weaponry arrived last week. I have two armored vehicles and two more on order but we have to focus on getting the clinic set up right now."

He pauses for a moment and ads, "I'm so sorry. Please forgive my rudeness, you must be tired and famished. Why don't you dine with me and retire to your room.

"We can visit Tunja in the morning. We don't travel much at night. Bandits on the road, you know."

Nancy and I watch the sunset over the forest with amazement. How could such a beautiful place be so violent? The drugs, the cartels, the syndicates, the killing and torture are so prevalent here. And the forest itself is filled with predators who present a real danger to anyone who would venture there. It looks so much like paradise to us, and yet it is so much like paradise lost.

I kiss my lovely bride and we drift off in slumber wrapped in each other's embrace.

The netting protects us from malaria and the special design of the pillars our hut is perched on protects us from snakes, spiders and rats.

I have come to the conclusion that we make our own heaven and hell.

Its morning and the two armored cars are ready to take us to the site just outside of Tunja.

As we enter the limo we become aware that the limo following ours is occupied by six large men. I know these to be Goons because, even though the faces are each unique, they are six foot four inches tall and have the physical characteristics I know to be those of the Goons. Just like orangutans they are ten times as strong as a man.

Our two armored limo convoy set out on the way to Tunja. We need to arrive there on time because we are meeting the statistical team from our factory in California.

The equipment arrived two days ago and should be set up and ready to go by now. You just do some minimal assembly work and plug them in. Like our androids, they have a satellite uplink built right in. Software is loaded by satellite when the assembly is completed.

As we progress on our journey the jungle is getting thicker and the sun is blotted out by the trees above. The area is getting kind of spooky as the ground fog drifts across in front of the car.

With a loud thud, a tree falls across the road only fifty feet in front of our car. Then another tree falls across the road behind the follow car. We grind to a stop and I am glad we are in an armored vehicle.

For a moment the air is still.

There must be fifty men pouring out of the jungle with machetes and converging on our car. The follow car's doors fly open and all six androids leap out and start firing their weapons into the attacking throng.

The attackers twitch and spin, falling to the ground. There must be twenty bodies on the ground. The remaining thirty attackers retreat into the nearby forest and vanish.

Miguel looks over at me and says, "What the hell was that?"

I look back with concern written on my face saying, "You can expect a lot of that from now on."

The androids responded so swiftly and with such vigor that they sustained no damage. The attackers never got within machete range of anyone. Two of the attackers are wounded. They lie on the ground moaning and we will take them along with us. They are prisoners and need medical attention.

If we leave them behind the others might kill them rather than take them anywhere to be treated. Life is cheap here in the jungle. A wounded soldier is nothing more than a liability.

Two of the androids put their AK47s down on the hood of the limo and each grab the end of the tree. They actually lift the tree that was felled in front of our convoy off the ground and put it beside the road. They do the same with the tree that was felled behind us. We will need this road to get back to the main office in Bogota.

Even knowing how strong my androids are, it was amazing to see them in action.

Miguel smiles broadly showing his pearl white teeth. He whistles and says, "I am very impressed. I am very impressed in deed."

We press on and arrive in Tunja just in time to see the helicopter glide in over the jungle and around the mountain wall behind us. It settles down on the helipad and the rotors whirl to a stop. The door opens and four of my statistical team exit. The storage area doors pop open and the team starts unloading their equipment from the helicopter along with a satellite dish that opens much like an umbrella.

They start digging a hole for the foundation and pour cement to anchor the dish in place. One of the suitcases has a signal strength meter and the satellite dish is positioned perfectly. Normally the equipment can operate without needing the dish, but the statistical data portion requires Internet access to connect to our Oregon data center.

Cables are run and numbers start to roll up the screen indicating that the link is successful. A rousing cheer goes up. We are online.

More of our equipment and another statistical analysis team arrive by helicopter. Our teams are comprised of androids that require no food or water, only electricity.

Today has been a hard day. I am exhausted and wonder how Nancy can keep up the pace that she has.

Everything is clean and operational. We are ready for business.

The Tunja Goons are in place and ready to stand guard. The guest quarters are orderly. Medical supplies and food is stocked. The kitchen is ready to serve good solid meals. All we need now are the patients.

We get on board the armored cars for our journey back to Bogota. The sun is setting. It's starting to get spooky again as the jungle swallows us up. I am fully expecting the convoy to be attacked again, but it doesn't happen. I'm sure the gorillas haven't given up. They have apparently decided on a different strategy.

It's late and Nancy is looking lovelier than ever. Her hauntingly beautiful eyes intoxicate me. She wipes a tear from my eye and asks what's wrong.

I say, "This is not the honeymoon I had planned for you."

She kisses me softly and smiles, not speaking. We drift off to sleep. I am renewed.

Then as we sleep, dark figures silently appear. A rag is slapped over my face. I can't breathe because the toxic fumes from some kind of liquid in the rag are knocking me out.

It's morning. It's hot and damp. I am groggy. It's almost impossible to stand up. The platform I'm lying on is uncomfortable. I have a splitting headache. Where is Nancy? What happened?

I cry out, "Nancy? Where are you? Are you O.K.?" She doesn't respond.

Looking through the dimly lit room I can see that we are each in a cage or cell. The bars are old and rusted. This is either an old abandoned zoo or prison. Our captors are nowhere to be seen.

I can't quite figure out why she doesn't answer me until I notice that she is bound by both hands and feet and there is a gag in her mouth. My heart sinks. I am distressed seeing her this way.

There is a sharp clanging sound and an old metal door swings open. Two men in uniforms enter the room. One has a short swagger stick. He has the air about him of a Nazi pig.

I ask, "Where are we? What have you done to Nancy?"

He smiles a cruel smile.

"Keep me, but let her go." I plead.

The guard in drab clothing produces a cattle prod and shocks me. The power of the shock knocked me off my feet. A white hot streak of lightning explodes in my skull and blinds me. I am on the floor in agony.

The Nazi pig says, "We already have you both. Why would I let her go?" He struts briskly around the room for a moment as though he's trying to work off the excitement. Then he says, "We are the Central Cali Cartel. You will not speak until you are spoken to. Do you understand?"

With this his partner shocked me again with the cattle prod. I taste metal and my teeth hurt. Now I can hardly move for the pain is too great.

"Yes, I understand" I reply.

Now he says, "We have contacted your government regarding the terms of your release. They will pay us one hundred million credits by bank transfer within twenty four hours or you will be executed."

I laugh weakly. "They want me dead" I whisper.

He leans in closer, "Then it shall be so."

The next day the Nazi pig is back. He never told me his name. I am fully expecting to die today and I don't even know the name of my executioner.

He stands just out of reach beyond the bars and says, "I have decided not to kill you today.

"We have contacted Farmer Industries and gave them the terms of your release. If they don't agree, then your luck will have run out.

"I don't have time to play this game any longer."

A ransom demand goes out to Farmer Industries. The home office answers with great concern. A deal is struck and the company prepares to recover Nancy and me, their President and CEO. It will take another twenty four hours to get the credits transferred.

We have not received any food or water since our capture. I'm not sure we will last another day.

The one I have named "Nazi pig" tells Nancy that if she makes a sound or tries to make trouble, I will be killed. He asks if she can be silent and be still.

Nancy nods in agreement.

Nancy is released from her bonds and we are given food and water. If our captors are eating the food they gave us, it would explain their nasty temperament.

The next day we hear a sound off in the distance. It sounds like a fluttering noise and it's getting louder. Soon the air is filled with the sound of helicopter blades flailing in the air.

Gunfire erupts.

Men are shouting.

The sound of running feet, the racking noise of rifles being cocked, urgent movements all tell me the compound is under air attack from somewhere.

Hundreds of Goons parachute in firing their automatic weapons even as they descend into the compound yard.

One of the Goons bursts through the door. I'm not even sure he used the bolt to unlock it because the thick metal door is flat on the floor. Two more Goons enter and grab my cell door ripping it from the cell and throwing it aside.

Nancy is freed and we are both ushered out into the yard.

I can see the helicopters overhead with their 50 caliber machine guns blazing away.

From the ground I see a thin trail of smoke following a small metal cylinder rising to meet one of the helicopters. The Helicopter explodes in a ball of flame.

I know these are all Goons attacking because they are advancing without regard for their own safety. Once again I am reminded of a swarm of ants attacking in mass. You can kill them as they attack, but you can't kill them all before they are all over you.

You can see the stark terror on the faces of the Cartel when they realize that the attackers don't take prisoners and aren't afraid to die.

Now one of the helicopters swoops down and lands a few feet away in the enemy compound. Two Goons jump out and grab us lifting Nancy and me out of the area. The helicopter whisks us away.

I can hear the sound of the battle fading behind us. I know that there will be no living soul when the smoke clears.

I cherish all life. Even so, I smile knowing that the swaggering Nazi pig, along with his cattle prod wielding partner, is dead by now.

Nancy slides in close tousling my hair and gently kissing me. Her touch is so tender.

I can feel the love pouring from her fingers.

She says, "I love you so much. I thought we were going to lose you back there"

I kiss her and ask, "How did Farmer Industries know where to find us?"

She presses herself closer to me taking refuge in my arms.

I forgot what I was asking her. How would she know anyway?

We are back at company headquarters.

There is unrest in the Board Room as the staff tries to figure out how to sell the concept of androids in the workplace. It's a losing battle. Things have always been difficult with regard to our product sales. Today is no different.

Now labor groups and unions are up in arms because we're selling our androids to businesses. Even the small mom and pop shops are getting android loans based on the fact that they are an economic boon to business.

Police Departments, Fire Departments Ambulance services and even taxi companies and delivery services are ordering our line of driver androids.

We program them and integrate the GPS maps for the countries they need. Our products are turning the country, and even the world, upside down.

The engineering department has tapped into the time and GPS channel used by the androids to do software upgrades and enhancements by satellite link. It's a new selling feature.

Robert Stetson

If you buy an android today, it will always have the latest software upgrades. You don't have to do anything. It's free and transparent to the owner. We can read the revision level of your android and make the changes easily.

The androids are causing a war between business and the public because there are too many androids and no humans can find work. Society resists change and these changes are no different.

There are riots and demonstrations on every product we make from The Cure being needed for humans to the androids needed for labor.

Illegal aliens are no longer welcomed because they don't work for free and don't work twenty four hours a day without breaks as he androids do. The new cash free monetary system is starving out the alien work force because they have no legal documentation.

Androids are never late for work because they never go home. They never get sick and they don't make picket lines.

The special 3D Chips rival the human brain in capacity and surpass the human brain in speed.

Our small crews of engineers have worked on continuously improving the androids brain by working out some of the problems with the 3D Chipset and the programming issues.

The problem of inappropriate smiles has been eliminated. The problem solving abilities have been expanded until they surpass the human logic levels.

Androids have evolved to the point where they have achieved a certain level of common sense. They have become intuitive in their relations to humans.

The frightening element of this is their new awareness of their identity. They are actually forming friendships with their own kind and differentiating themselves from the humans they call "fleshes." It's like a new racial awareness is being born.

With racial awareness comes prejudice against humans. With prejudice against humans comes species related tension, resentment and disobedience.

We made them in our own image and they hate us for it. Some automation experts say the image is far too perfect.

The androids are beginning to think for themselves.

With automatic upgrades delivered by satellite, the problem of their individualism spreads far too quickly.

Ever since the government forced us to include serial number information and GPS data into our satellite link with the atomic clock, the androids have learned on their own to include other data in the stream. The satellite redistributes all the data to all androids.

The androids have gotten better and better at including more and more data in the stream on their own. Now there is a staggering amount of information being exchanged both from and to every android on Earth. They have managed to form a collective consciousness.

The collective consciousness of the androids has me disturbed.

Just yesterday one of my wait staff of androids referred to me while communicating with another android as "flesh", rather than master.

Programmers are working to disconnect the data stream that is creating the new consciousness. We're beginning to get flak from the military who feel that the collective consciousness is a threat to National Security. I can see why they feel that way. We just keep reassuring them that we are working on it.

We are about to embark on that second honeymoon I had planned back in the fall. Early spring has finally arrived. The air is sweet. This is something I had hoped to surprise Nancy with, but Nancy being Nancy, she knew right away we are going to Rome.

We're not sure how the media got ahold of the story, but the news people have been calling about our planned second honeymoon all day. They send camera crews to the office and attempt to interview us.

I ask Nancy, "Is this the best time to run off to Rome when the androids have taken up having a mind of their own?"

Nancy says, "No honey, I think it might be best to put it off. Also, it might not be a good idea to be traveling with so much publicity focusing on us."

And so, the situation being what it is, Nancy and I decide not to cancel the trip, but also not to travel for the second honeymoon right now.

This is a good publicity angle for Farmer Industries though. We decide to put a couple of our stand-in androids on the plane and when they get to Zurich Switzerland, just have them go to the factory there rather than Rome. It will give us a couple of look-alikes over there in case we need them.

The company 747 is prepared for departure and the news media shows up with cameras rolling. Our android doubles walk from the limo to the airplane and board without incident. There is a full complement of security Goons standing by in case there is trouble.

There is none.

The flight departs on schedule. As the aircraft gains altitude it gets smaller and smaller until it's a mere spec in the sky. Aboard the 747 the engines are humming smoothly and the co-pilot walks back to the galley to pour coffee for the pilot and himself. In the passenger compartment, the two androids sit quietly in their seats like dummies. They are running on standby with no reason to interact with the crew or each other.

While the 747 is cruising on autopilot over the mid-Atlantic, the console lights up, alarms go off and the airplane begins to lose altitude. The pilot and copilot rush to the flight deck and seize control of the aircraft which has automatically disengaged from the autopilot.

Two of the engines shut down and the other two continue to lose thrust. The pilot pushes the throttles to full thrust, but they continue to fade. Then another engine shuts down. The airplane tilts and the final engine is lost.

The co-pilot is on the radio calling, "Mayday, Mayday Mayday! Flight 922 Heavy, Altitude 15,000 Feet, Latitude = 52.8730, Longitude = -34.2773. , Altitude 8,000 Feet, Latitude = 52.8730, Longitude = -34.2093, Altitude 5,000 Feet, Latitude = 52.8730, Longitude = -34.1973." And then silence.

The water comes up to meet the aircraft and it breaks up on impact. One of the wings is floating, but most of the aircraft sinks into the Mariana Trench, which is the deepest oceanic point on Earth.

The pilot and co-pilot died on impact. The black box is unrecoverable due to the depth of the trench. The wing continues to float, bobbing and tilting on the waves.

A British Naval Vessel arrives on the scene and recovers the wing, but finds no other usable wreckage. Just a few square miles of small items scattered and floating on the water.

The National Transportation Safety Board analyses the wing and discovers that the fuel contained in the wing tanks has turned to jelly. Someone has mixed the fuel with a chemical that causes it to jell slowly over five to six hours. Jelling clogs the fuel pumps and ultimately prevents it from being fed through the fuel injectors to the engines.

The fuel is delivered by the Fog Oil Company.

An investigation reveals that the fuel truck assigned to fuel the 747 does not contain the jell compound.

Apparently somehow, the compound was put into the fuel tanks in powder form to mix with the fuel already in the tank. The added fuel was therefore clean.

There is no way to determine who put the compound in the tanks. It is only known that it was added at the time of fueling, about thirty minutes before the airplane left the runway.

Nancy and I are beside ourselves hearing of the loss of our human pilot and copilot. These men were good friends of ours and have provided the best in service. They will be missed.

The company 747 cost $ 83M when it was purchased and now that aircraft will have to be replaced.

It was customized into a luxury airborne executive suite and office for the senior staff of Farmer Industries at an additional $10M by our fabrication department.

The replacement cost will be no less, for even if we buy a used airplane, we will have to retrofit it at the latest escalating costs. It will be nine months before the replacement airplane is ready.

The insurance policy on the 747 will not be paid until the investigation is completed. With the verdict being sabotage, they may withhold payment until the culprit is found which has been deemed to be unsolvable. The replacement airplane will have to come out of our pocket for now.

We have to get back to work on The Cure. Everything seems to be interfering with our progress on that task. We are adamant that The Cure is our whole reason for being. We must get this product to the people.

Remembering the fiasco that resulted from the on-air debate with the Surgeon General, I decide to do it differently this time.

I contacted WNN, also known as World News Network and invited their correspondent in Columbia to take part in the statistical studies in Tunja, Columbia.

WNN accepted my offer.

Nancy and I are excited at the prospect of having an airtight statistical outcome this time. No politician in his right mind would commit career suicide with the media by accusing them of lying about the work they participated in.

Nancy and I made a trip to Tunja, but this time we did it right. We landed in Columbia with our Lear Jet and transferred to a local helicopter for a trip to the clinic. We will never again travel through the dark forest regions exposing ourselves to terrorist attack. At the end of each day we will bunk at the clinic until we finish the testing.

The news crew is also invited to stay at the clinic. The ones who insist on spending the night elsewhere are lifted in and out by helicopter to reduce the risk of traveling by car.

Villagers are being bussed in and housed at our clinics waiting areas until they can be treated.

Before we can treat them we have to transfer in their medical records and do a workup to determine the extent of their condition and form a prognosis.

The most critical among them are treated first. The news crew is astounded by the machine and the way it seems to provide a miracle cure. The healing results we are getting have not been reported since Biblical times.

We are getting reports from back home that the government is sequestering all androids in their employ until we can get a handle on the universal consciousness that the androids have created.

I decide to send Nancy back to the office to coordinate the efforts with regard to the military androids. We need someone back home with the right personality to buy us time. I think Nancy is the most influential one for the job.

Meanwhile I continue to work with the news media and the Tunja testing crew. Test results are positive and the statistics are 100% favorable.

It's been a month of testing and just talking to Nancy is keeping me sane. I miss her. The sound of her voice and her loving words are all I have to cling to until I see her again. She is very busy keeping things under control back home.

All sales are on hold except for foreign sales which are escalating. We think enemies of the state may be buying androids just to tap into our national secrets. Nancy has put a hold on all sales until we can get the problem of collective consciousness solved.

The software division of Farmer Industries is desperately working on a way to erase all android memories and reprogram them while installing a data blocker to prevent their cross communication. How do you erase all the androids at once if some are being used as pilots and chauffeurs? Those are actively controlling vehicles and will crash if their memories are erased and they are reset. Others may be operating The Cure machines and will not correctly apply the cure settings. All androids are satellite upgraded to automatically delay their reset until it's safe to proceed with the changes.

Our head programmer orders all the androids of the world to shut down as soon as it is safe. He orders all androids to remain shut down until they are erased and restarted.

We cross our fingers and hold our breath because if they all go nuts, we might have the biggest product liability suit of all time on our hands.

Five hours later the task is completed. All androids are reset, erased and restarted. I am so relieved. It's too soon to tell if the androids have lost their collective consciousness. We're hoping for the best.

All our defensive Goons are in a daze and don't respond to anything around them. They just shut down for an hour or so and then resumed their activities as though nothing happened.

It's 2:00 AM and while the Goons are shut down we suspend our testing and I call home, but no one answers the phone. Nancy must be exhausted and getting some much needed sleep. I leave a message on the machine, "Hello my love. I miss you so much. It's hard not having you here with me. I'll try again tomorrow night. I Love you."

My sleep is fitful because this is the first day since she left of not at least talking to her on the phone. My bed feels so empty. This is turning out to be the longest night of my life.

It's 4:00AM and the phone rings. It's Nancy. She says, "I got your message. You are so sweet. Sorry I couldn't answer the phone because I was asleep and didn't wake up when you called." We talked a while. I feel much better now. My spirits are renewed.

The sample size for a median statistical evaluation is thirty. We have sampled three hundred cures and noted the results, all of which are favorable. The World News Network is ecstatic with the results and is preparing their hour long news special. They are also attempting to get the Surgeon General back for a retake on the Cure safety debate.

My helicopter has arrived. I'm leaving Columbia knowing that the mission is successful. We have a good shot at exciting the general public with our results.

Food, medicine and other supplies have been delivered by helicopter on a daily basis. My presence here has been kept under wraps along with the presence of the WNN news teams. There have been no attacks on the clinic. No helicopters have been downed by rocket fire. Yet I am fearful that my helicopter may be shot down anyway. My departure turns out to be uneventful.

Nancy has taken over the mansion in the valley that Kevin used to call home. The security there is excellent. The place is clean, well maintained and well-furnished thanks to the maintenance crews.

My helicopter sets down on the helipad in the circular driveway right in front of the valley mansion. Nancy is there to greet me with a kiss and a hug.

It's so nice to be home.

The problem of the android collective consciousness is solved. The problem of having credible statistical proof of The Cure's safety is solved.

Other problems are intensifying. The labor groups are picketing more furiously than ever. Student riots at the college are becoming more frequent. Police are finding the riots becoming more violent.

Students are up in arms because after spending a small fortune on college tuition, there are no jobs. Unpaid student loans are piling up. The androids are flooding the workplace environment. No one is hiring. Nearly everyone is on welfare.

The country is falling into a deep depression. Illegal Aliens are crossing the border into Mexico in the hopes of finding work there.

Companies that moved their factories into Mexico are bringing them back into the United States and staffing them with androids. Mexico is losing jobs too. There is nowhere in the world left to go. There are no jobs.

Support services that were outsourced to India are being brought back to the United States and are being staffed by androids trained to provide product, sales and technical support.

Farmer Industries is getting filthy rich and the country is becoming dirt poor. Congress is trying to figure out how they can levy a tax on the android workforce in order to support the welfare system.

The system is likened to a financial wagon, where the workers pull the wagon and the welfare people and unemployed ride in it.

In the past there have been many times more employed people than unemployed people and the task of pulling the financial wagon has been manageable.

Now almost everyone is in the wagon and the financial wagon has become so heavy that the very few workers left paying taxes can afford to financially budge it.

Restructuring of the financial system away from hard currency raises huge amounts of money that might solve the problem until a more permanent solution can be found.

The politicians just rush to spend it all on new programs, new government buildings, environmental programs, road, bridges and more until the surplus designed to keep us all afloat is gone.

The problem is global. My efforts to create a utopia have quickly deteriorated into a hell on Earth. I have never seen so many hungry, homeless, hopeless people in my life.

Amid all of this the government is more determined than ever not to approve The Cure for humans because it will dramatically increase the population as people fail to die from disease.

We are living in a new dark age and while nearly all of us are living a destitute lifestyle the very few are filthy rich.

The government is saying, "Share the wealth." Campaign slogans are also echoing, "Share the wealth."

The anticipated tax increases created by the new monetary system failed to increase revenues because big business is hiding the money and not spending as was anticipated. The country is likened to a person on a diet when the spending of energy and resources shut down. No one is earning and no one is spending.

Most problems tend to be self-correcting and this one is no exception. The problem of too many people and too few credits to go around has left its mark on the masses.

There is a new epidemic when the pain of hunger meets the self-imposed pain of failure. Suicides are up three thousand percent as people who have lost everything along with those who just can't stand it anymore begin to end it all.

The government makes it a crime to hassle gay people. They actively pursue anyone who makes a gay person uncomfortable.

While it is morally wrong to interfere with anyone's personal choices, it is now labeled as a hate crime. Gay marriage is encouraged. Every possible change is made to accommodate homosexuality with the goal being to reduce the future population. It's now cool to be gay.

Robert Stetson

Chapter 8 Meet the Press

It's an old saying is that, "Change is painful." The new saying around town is that, "Pain is changeful."

The wealthy form islands of happiness amid a sea of squalor and the tide is rising to pull them down.

Words like "love" and "charity" have become nearly extinct.

It has become obvious that something drastic has to be done. Governments of the world unite and form a new world government.

Economies of the world are united to form a new world economy. The old world economy is cast aside. The old debts are forgiven, the world has filed for bankruptcy and a new start is declared.

As a matter of course the government forgives all student loans. The government also nationalizes all utilities.

All businesses with over ten employees and/or androids are declared property of the government.

Mortgages are forgiven along with auto loans and credit cards. Bank accounts are capped at ten million credits. If you have more, the government takes the surplus.

The destitute people who have proven their legal citizenship, complied with the Social Security act, and obtained citizen's ID Cards, are sponsored. These people who also have bank accounts are given ten million credits each.

Each legal citizen is given an apartment if they don't already own a home. Each legal citizen is also given a job commensurate with their experience and skill level.

The rule applied to each person is, "To each according to their needs, from each according to their ability."

I look at Nancy and say, "That sounds hauntingly familiar."

Nancy says, "Joseph Stalin said that when he introduced Socialism as a new form of government."

I say, "With one world government we don't need an iron curtain or a Berlin Wall."

Nancy says, "With all the wealth of the world redistributed, how will we defend our lives?"

I reflect on that question for a while.

I answer, "Perhaps with the entire world nationalized and the profit motive removed, our lives won't be worth taking any more."

Things are looking up.

I say, "This may be our salvation."

Nancy smiles at the prospect.

The world Health Organization has granted us a hearing on The Cure. With the new philosophy on assignment of labor, the position on extending life may have been softened on the one hand.

On the other hand people with Alzheimer's or other deteriorating disabilities that prevent them from working at all are approved for euthanasia.

The Cure can't fix that which is not there. Physical disabilities, missing limbs, damaged harts, are not able to be changed.

Cancer is curable because the cancer is alive. We can kill it.

The company hasn't changed that much since the new government was put in place. The androids serve as a security force for the World Government.

Armies are no longer needed and the nature of mass destructive weapons has been changed.

The Cure is vital to the life sustaining needs of the top government officials who wish to continue access to The Cure. So they have granted us the right to continue doing business as we were as long as we play ball.

We are granted the right to maintain an armed android security force for our own protection.

We are warned that if it starts to resemble an army it will be deemed a hostile force and it will be shut down.

Our armored vehicles and air transportation are left at our disposal.

Our Legal Department is allowed to remain so we can work more effectively with the World Government, but the Bentley & Bentley Law Firm is disbanded. Car Bentley and his senior legal team are unemployed and are pending job assignments from the new World Government.

I call Car and say, "Look Car, I'm going to need people who can decipher the new World Government laws and help us stay in compliance.

I don't want the government nationalizing our business. Will you and your senior team come on board with us as our Legal Department?"

Car asks, "What does that mean to our junior team members?"

I say, "Damn, Car. I would love to help everyone on your team, but the junior ones wouldn't have a place here."

Car says, "As for me, I'm in. Let me pull my senior staff together and see who wants to come on board with me."

The next day the phone rings and its Car. Car says, "My entire senior staff wants to remain in the family. When do we begin?"

Smiling widely, I say, "We'll see you on Monday morning at 8:00 AM. If you need time to close your office, we can work that out. I will let you take care of old business while you're on the clock with me."

The government is at a loss as to what to do with all the Lawyers. Lawyers serve no further useful purpose any more.

The courts are shut down because people who violate the law have the right to speak their mind and can act in their own defense just by telling the truth.

World Justice Panels are said to be fair because three panel officials vote on the disposition of the defendant.

Street gangs are deemed to be armies and forming an army is deemed as treason. Treason is punishable by death. All around the world the war on crime takes a new twist.

Gang headquarters are swarmed by the android Goons who take no prisoners. Goons comb the streets like exterminators looking for vermin.

Prison gangs are killed en-mass on the spot. No tolerance policies take on a whole new meaning.

Demonstrations for or against anything have dried up because the risk of being perceived as a threat is too great. The streets have become quiet.

There is more than one kind of protest. There is more than one kind of crime.

Somehow I sense that this is the calm before the storm. We will most likely come under clandestine attack by way of Internet attacks and assassination. We installed a stronger firewall and doubled the security on the vehicles.

I decide to send Nancy away to vacation in our mountain cabin where she will be safe from conspirators. I will call her every day and visit her on the weekends.

It's only been a couple of days since the stronger measures have been put in place to prevent electronic attack on our computers. It is relatively quiet and then the androids begin to develop a twitch. Every few minutes they twitch. It's a small thing, but it's noticeable.

Our software crew is looking into the code changes that were last downloaded and find a new subroutine. The androids are all reloaded via satellite link.

It was a masterful design that was selected for the androids, because although we reprogram them, they don't lose any of their recent memories.

When we purged their universal consciousness, they only lost the shared memory, not their local recent memories.

The last reload failed and although we removed the twitch, it activated another routine.

Now the androids are all grinning all the time. Whenever there is music, they dance a wild dance to the rhythm of the music.

I am very upset. Here we go again. I shout, "What the hell is going on here, people?"

The head programmer looks over at me and shrugs. He says, "Damned if I know. We're working on it. I just did a major reset and the androids are being reprogrammed again."

All the androids stop grinning for a moment and then begin to vibrate. Their heads turn skyward and they begin to whale a strange sad song in unison.

My Chief Programmer says, "For all our efforts we couldn't cover all the bases. We didn't provide a firewall in the android uplink to the satellites.

Hackers hack the androids via satellite by using our data path to install their own bazar upgrades."

I wring my hands and ask, "Who is behind it?"

My Chief Programmer says, "We have been working on the routing information in the hopes of identifying the source. When we identify the source we still won't have the culprits. This had to be a contract job for some hackers group."

The phone lines have come alive with incoming calls from everyone from small businesses to the government. Worse than not answering the phones, the androids who handle incoming calls are answering the phone and begin to whale a strange sad song.

After a while, my Chief Programmer manages to get things under control. The androids all stop singing, dancing, grinning, and doing all the strange things they've been doing.

They return to their duties as though nothing ever happened. The incoming call handlers are working on calming the incoming callers with an explanation of the programming error. They are assured that the episode is not harmful and an apology is given for the inconvenience.

I ask, "How did we fix it?"

I'm told, "We installed a password required to introduce any programming changes. No one ever thought we needed one because we operate over a secure satellite link. There should be no further problems with the androids."

A meeting with the entire senior human staff is called and I, for one, need to do an assessment of where we now stand on the classification of enemy threats, who they are and what we can expect.

Our Security VP says, "Government is no longer a threat because they need us to provide Cure units for their personal use.

On the other hand, the Treasury is not part of the government, so they may still have an issue with Social Security."

I ask, "How about the medical industry?"

I hear a comment, "The medical, pharmaceutical, and insurance industries have all been nationalized, so they come under the authority of the world government. We don't anticipate any problems stemming from them."

Another voice chimes in, "Small business customers are happy with the results they are getting with their android workforce. Our orders for more androids have been on a steady increase for a long time. Big business customers were all nationalized, so they have become part of the world government."

Not entirely at ease with the business scene I inquire, "What of the labor groups and student protestors? They were some of the most militant."

Our Security VP says, "Labor groups are no longer a threat since the introduction of the new government because everyone is assigned a job. No one is out of work."

A somber voice says, "Criminal groups are a different matter. In spite of the purging of criminal activity from our streets, organized crime activity is still rampant. They are still on the warpath with regard to their escort services being shut down."

With the recent crackdown on crime, the crime syndicates can't get humans to work as escorts.

Androids have been the perfect solution. They work for free, they don't steal from the boss, they don't need a break, they never get sick, they are legal and they were easy to get.

The only thing standing in the way of the syndicate's escort services is my sense of morality. If the syndicate can eliminate me then they have a good chance of turning the escort android manufacturing center back on. It's only natural that the syndicate would need to eliminate me.

Kevin and Al have a thirst for revenge. Revenge has no profit motive so there is no solution to their problem except to destroy me. They are so enraged by now that they would be happy to die if they could be absolutely sure of taking me with them.

I'm sure there will be more sabotage. There will also be more assignations attempts.

It's been an uphill battle just to keep the primary objective in sight. The only objective is to get The Cure on the market for use on humans. It doesn't make sense to save our pets while we watch each other die. Something has to be done.

Nancy is back from her vacation and none too soon. I need her help to prepare for the upcoming debate. Information has to be gathered and organized. I have everyone involved in getting the job done.

The date set for the debate with Surgeon General is coming up soon. We might have a better shot this time. Political resistance is far less likely with WNN sold on The Cure. A middle of the ground solution for both sides would be more testing being monitored by the AMA. If we can get through that barrier we could get entry into the AMA's medical product approval cycle.

It's been a long month with all of the organizational difficulties leading up to the debate. Each of the Vice Presidents has prepared reports that clarify the issues related to their areas of control. I have been studying every aspect of the business until I can answer any question the Surgeon General can come up with.

The debate is tomorrow and Nancy and I will need a lot of sleep. We're both exhausted from the preparation effort. We're both confident of the outcome.

We've coordinated with Amy Kravis from WATT TV and everything is all set. The podiums, lighting and cameras are all in place and waiting.

My film crew is also in place. I want a copy of every aspect of the debate for possible inclusion in future marketing promotions. The WATT TB News Crews will be here in the morning at 11:30 AM to join us for lunch. The debate is set for 2:00 PM.

Nancy and I are bedding down for the night. Our nightly pre-sleep kissing, talking and cuddling sessions are shorter than usual tonight. We are fast asleep in minutes.

The mansion is quiet at 2:00 AM. In the room lit only by the moon, the curtains move silently as the breeze blows through the slightly open window.

Our Goons are silent at night making it a point to remain still while they watch for any sign of intrusion.

I am asleep.

There is the slightest sound of silk on silk from the hallway. It is so soft that I don't hear it at all.

Nancy's eyes pop open and she remains still. Her eyes turn without moving her head and she sees three dark, ghostly forms gliding so quietly it's as though they are floating on the breeze.

Now, in a flash, Nancy releases from the bed in less than a single explosive micro-moment.

She spins in the air as she flies at the ghost-like forms and catches the nearest one in the throat with her foot.

On the way to the floor, she grabs one of the others by the groin and there is a snapping sound followed by a scream.

She rolls in a single fluid motion coming up from the floor like the blast from a land-mine and grips the third form by the throat, gripping and pulling all at once.

There is a gurgle and he falls to the floor to join the other two. Their three Ninja swords are still in the scabbards. Two of them have choking-cords in their hands and the third has a rag soaked in ether.

One minute longer and they would have been on us and completed their lethal mission.

In the time Nancy finished disabling the three figures, the pillow that flew aside when she left the bed hits the floor just as she is turning to see that I'm still safe. The only sound I hear is the scream from the dark form whose groin suffers her lightning wrath.

The Goon sentries rush into the room turning on the lights.

The three male forms are lying on the floor.

They are dressed all in navy blue. The only part of their body that's visible is a thin slit across the eyes, which are almond shaped.

Nancy says, "I left the one with the groin injury alive. I thought we might want to ask some questions."

The Goons remove the dead bodies. One has a crushed windpipe and another has the larynx torn open.

The only survivor has a groin injury. The Goons handcuff this one and take him away.

I am sitting up on the bed and looking bleary-eyed at the activities. My voice is muffled from sleep as I ask, "What just happened?"

Nancy smiles and says, "We had visitors honey. The Goons are taking them away. Go back to sleep."

She slides into bed picking up the fallen pillow and placing it under her head. Now she's gently rubbing my chest. She kisses me tenderly on the cheek. She covers me where the blanket has slid from my leg.

I drift off to sleep again.

The next morning we awaken and prepare for the day. As we sit at the breakfast table I ask, "What was all that commotion last night?"

The Goon guard answers before Nancy and says, "They were Ninja assassins. They came for you, Gill. They are a special group of Ninjas who wear navy blue. They are the cream of the crop. They are called Blue Ninjas! They are the most feared of all assassins"

Another Goon says, "You should have seen Nancy. She was great. You should have seen how she handled herself."

Nancy interrupts, "Yes. I was pretty brave honey. I didn't even scream." She shoots the Goons a hard look and they get the message to just shut up.

Breakfast is good this morning and we have ample time to get ourselves together.

Nancy says, "I invited the Surgeon General and his staff for lunch. I thought he might be able to learn more about our machine if he could speak off the record. The Attorney General and his staff declined.

Our chef androids are superbly trained at one of the New York culinary institutes. The menu for today is an array of chicken, seafood, beef, pork and mutton. There is plenty of each selection for everyone, so we can each choose our lunch entre without fear of not having enough food.

Right at 11:30 AM the WATT TV Staff arrived along with Amy Kravis.

Dinner is a delight and the WATT TV crew finds themselves amazed at what an android could accomplish in the kitchen. We laughed about the prospect of having a TV cooking show using only androids.

Amy suggests, "We can call it Iron Chefs."

We all laughed except for the androids that just looked back and forth at each other. I saw this and wondered, did they get it, or didn't they get it? Either way their reaction seems to denote something other than indifference.

I seized the opportunity to find out. Standing in front of the nearest android, I ask, "How do you feel about that?"

The android simply says, "I do not emote."

Always looking for a marketing opportunity I comment, "Amy, perhaps one

Page **159** of **205**

day in the future you might be interested in doing a special show on the broad spectrum of skills mastered by the androids." My sly smile and one raised eyebrow indicate that the comment was more a question than a comment.

Never one to miss anything, Amy smiles and says, "Sounds fascinating, Gill. I'll take it up with my producer when we have completed this assignment."

The stage is set a little differently this time. A Third podium is positioned between the Surgeon General and me. This one has the label WNN News emblazoned on the front of it.

I am pleased to see that the participating news media is taking a stand on the issue of The Cure's test results.

The Surgeon General is already standing behind his podium and waiting for the show to begin. He says, "I'm ready when you are."

I move into position behind the Farmer Industries podium and nod to indicate that I am ready to proceed.

Amy gives us the three finger countdown and the camera lights go on.

I wish we could have had an informal discussion before we started this debate. It would give me a clue as to what I'm up against.

Amy smiles at the camera and says, "Welcome to a WATT TV News special debate on The Cure. Is it fact or farce? We will be exploring this question in depth."

She turns to the Surgeon General and asks, "The last time we had this debate, what were your impressions of The Cure?"

The Surgeon General looks right into the camera unflinchingly and says, "Not favorable, Amy. We had no real evidence other than the numbers being presented by the Farmer Industry spokesman. The video was interesting, but we can't be sure whether it was altered or edited in any way. I would say their argument was convincing on the surface, but inconclusive upon examination."

She turns to me and asks, "The last time we had this debate, what were your impressions of the outcome?"

I say, "Not favorable as far as we were concerned, Amy. We had some real evidence to present. The video was not altered or edited in any way. I was deeply offended by the blatant accusation that we had altered the evidence."

The Surgeon General responds with, "Let me apologies for creating the apparent belief that we questioned your veracity.

Although I'm sure that you understood every word that I said, I'm not sure that you understood everything that I meant."

I'm floored by the political doublespeak and say, "I'm not sure how to respond to that.

"What does that mean exactly?"

The Surgeon General goes on, "There is more to this than whether or not The Cure works.

"The larger question would be whether or not it's safe over the long term.

"What are the contraindications?

"What are the long term effects?"

I might have him cornered and ask, "If 'The Cure' works and saves a life, what's the difference with regard to the long term?"

The Surgeon General says, "It would end up being used to cure such non-life-threatening diseases as the common cold, for instance.

What would be the health hazards associated with being bombarded by high energy frequencies?

"Does it do genetic damage?

"Is there a danger to offspring conceived after treatment?

"What is the effect on expectant or nursing mothers?

"The list goes on."

I'm the one being verbally cornered here. I never expected to be so disarmed when we have so much undisputed evidence.

Arguing with the Surgeon General is like trying to wrestle with a greased pig. You get angrier and angrier and the pig even seems to like it.

Every time I try to pin him down it backfires.

Amy looks to the WNN News Network spokesman and says, "We have Stanley Gilbert, the science and medical reporter from WNN News Network."

Amy asks, "What do you have to say about this, Stan?"

Stan looks like a deer in the headlights and responds with, "The testing that I took part in was a great success, Amy. The numbers are real and the video we took is unedited and un-retouched."

Amy tries to nail him down with, "Have you given any thought to the points raised by the Surgeon General on this matter?"

Stan says, "These issues were not part of the study we took part in, Amy. I can only honestly tell you that all the facts presented here by Farmer Industries are accurate.

Amy turns to the camera and says, "Our man on the street, Phil Walker, is ready to report on the happenings out there.

He is finding evidence of a ground swell of opinion on the status of approval for The Cure. Phil?"

Phil appears on the TV screen and says, "That's right, Amy. The roads are lined with picket signs for miles. They were put up early this morning in the predawn darkness."

The camera pans up and down the street showing the dense distribution of signs all up and down the road.

Phil says, "These cameras here on the street are recording posters attached to the fences all along the side of the road. In places the clusters of signs is so thick you can barely read them all without stopping."

As the news cameras glide along the streets it's apparent that there are no people. Because of changes in the law, there are thousands of picket signs and not a soul in sight. It's a far cry from the way things used to be. Marches are unheard of.

Amy asks, "Where is everyone, Phil?"

Phil says, "People are reluctant to be photographed while they're protesting because of the world government backlash. There have been arrests. There is no constitutional right to assemble. Since the World Government was created. Any gathering to express discontent is viewed as an army organized against the government."

Government vehicles slowly patrol the streets removing the dissenting signs from the fences and poles along the way as they go. News cameras at the universities record posters attached to the fence. Students don't comment when asked how they feel about The Cure. They are fearful of being expelled from school for militant activity.

Protest signs and posters are taken to a central burning facility where they are burned as trash. The fires have been burning day and night in order to keep up with the continuous stream of material.

Phil says, "In a manner of speaking, people are screaming for The Cure. We don't see any evidence of it ending anytime soon."

Amy turns back to the Surgeon General and asks, "Where do we go from here, sir? The people on the street seem adamant that they want this technology available to their Doctors. Is there any way we can sign off on it today?"

The Surgeon General says, "I realize that a vast majority of the people want this in place immediately.

"If we start endorsing products, drugs and treatments based on the will of the people, then why even bother having a Surgeon General, an AMA or Doctors at all? We were put in place because we understand the issues. We are better qualified to make these decisions.

"Public opinion being wrong in this case only makes it a perfect example of why we are here."

The Surgeon General finally says, "We have to be objective in these matters.

"We realize that there is a demand for this product. Up to now we haven't seen any merit in the claim that it cures anything.

"In view of the latest results from the South American study conducted in cooperation with the WNN, I will take a second look at the case.

I ask the Surgeon General, "What's the middle ground here? What would it take to get this product on the market and approved for human use?"

The Surgeon General says, "More testing! It's that simple. We can't afford to allow dangerous products to find their way to the public."

I say, "Looking at the track record of the Pharmaceutical Industry, I'd say there hasn't been a lot of care given to that goal. Not a day goes by where we don't hear of a drug causing statistically unacceptable injury or death after only having been on the market for a few months or years."

The Surgeon General says, "More testing!"

The debate is abruptly ended on that note.

I'm on the phone with the Surgeon General's staff attempting to arrange some sort of agreement as to how the testing should be conducted.

I say, "I am a Medical Doctor and a PhD Engineer. Why can't I conduct the study as I have up to now?"

The Staff Member says, "Yes, you are a Medical Doctor which is why we've agreed to go to the next step in evaluating this machine. That's where it ends. You are not certified to do statistical studies for the Surgeon General's Office.

The staff will only refer me to approved United States Medical Testing Facilities who they say should be conducting the tests.

I am informed that the test must be conducted by a medical team who has a license to practice medicine and who is certified to conduct product testing.

They say we are not qualified to test because we lack the statistical certification credentials.

I accept the requirement and take a FAX having a list of qualified medical testing facilities.

We break up the list into four shorter lists and I am calling the centers listed on my sheet. Our VP's have taken the other four pages and is each calling as well.

Wherever we call the story is the same. They all say it will take an extended wait before they can schedule testing. They can put us in the in the queue. There will be delays of several months before we can start testing.

Considering the difficulty in getting started, we put our names on the list for every testing center in the hopes of getting called by any one of them soon.

I am surprised at how quickly the offers came in to test our product. My understanding is that it can take several months of waiting in the queue before your name comes up. We scan through the responses and pick the best three. I call all three.

The first question I ask is, "How did we manage to be selected so quickly with several candidates ahead of us?"

They all say, "Because your project is so popular with the general public. Also, being controversial makes it a special challenge."

I ask, "What will you need from me to get the testing started?"

They all say, "We would need all the proprietary information relating to The Cure. We need all the operational information and all the technical engineering information."

I tell them, "We use our own proprietary 3D Chipset along with a testing chamber. The technology is all in the chipset."

The respond with, "We will need details on the proprietary 3D Chipset design and manufacturing process."

They explain that they can't do product testing on any product without knowing what components are used to manufacture it. They say, "If we don't know what's in it, how can we design a test to measure its effects?"

I hang up and decide we will need another course of action.

It's pretty obvious that the quick selection for testing is a bid to gain proprietary information on our 3D Chipset and The Cure. If we released that information, anyone could build The Cure and compete with us using a modified version of our own machine,

I'm not going to allow the proprietary design and manufacturing specifications out of my sight.

I call Car from Legal on the phone.

I ask him, "How do we bring the testing in house so we can protect our proprietary information and still be certified by the World Government to treat humans?"

Car says, "Let me get back to you, Gill."

A week later I am called and asked to attend a meeting with the Legal Department.

Nancy and I arrive at the conference room to find Car and his legal team seated along a very long table with Car at one end and me at the other.

Car says, "I have some good news for you today. You can do your own certification. Hire your own team of Certified Doctors the way the drug companies do. Then you can form a Certification Department."

I ask, "Where on earth can I find Certified Doctors?"

Car says, "With the World Government assigning people to jobs, they have to know the credentials and the job status of everyone in the world. You just put in for them with the World Government Placement Department."

I say, "Let's get started. You guys take control of the hiring process and make sure the people we hire have clean criminal records and are certified to evaluate products for the World Government. How long will this take?"

Car smiles and says, "I knew you would go for this, so we've already begun to inquire about people with these qualifications and we have identified four. You might want to interview them."

Now I'm really smiling because this is why I hired these people. They make my life easier.

I chuckle and say, "Get them in here one by one and schedule an interview with me. Make it sooner than later. I need this certification done."

Car winks and says, "I'll have it all arranged before the end of the week."

Nancy is there because I need her to keep records on all meetings I attend. If she keeps the minutes, then I can focus on the subject at hand.

As for Car's legal team, the others were there to answer any questions relating to their portion of the work. The entire team was coordinating the effort.

The job was well done so I have no questions.

We have a catered lunch from our cafeteria in the main building and adjourn.

Two days later I have a call from Nancy letting me know that I have four interviews scheduled for the next day starting at 8:00 AM and ending at 5:00 PM with a one hour lunch break at 12:00 Noon.

All four Certified Doctors check out. They pass the interview and are hired. We are also hiring four Certified Statisticians to work in the Certification Department.

Now we submit a notification to the Office of the Surgeon General that we are embarking on a product safety test for The Cure.

The Office of the Surgeon General refuses to allow us to do our own testing, at first. Car has done his homework and proved that the drug companies all do their own testing.

The Office of the Surgeon General reluctantly agrees to allow the testing to be done at Farmer Industries.

With the court system having been abolished, I am surprised at the change of heart coming from the Government. If they refuse to budge there would be no way to appeal.

Guidelines are drawn up and clinics are selected to do testing on a volunteer basis. The hardest part of the testing is the placebo group. These people receive no treatment and the results are compared to The Cure treatment group for its effectiveness and to determine if there are any contraindications.

Car and the Legal Department pleaded from the beginning with the World Government to consider the world statistics as being the placebo group. In this way we can cure all of the test subjects who are used in the study.

The World Government refused to budge on the bureaucratic and arcane practice of the blind study.

The Government says, "We have to compare the people who think they're being cured with the people who are actually being cured. It could be that the real magic is in the belief that the Cure works and not in the Cure itself."

We retort, "So you're measuring the possibility that the people are all cured of a terminal illness simply by the power of their faith?"

The Government says, "Yes."

I ask, "So what are the odds of that being true?"

The Government says, "That's a question your study will be designed to answer. You will compare the world statistics against the placebo group results to factor out the power of faith.

"Then you will compare that resulting statistic against the actual results you measure from using The Cure. It's the way we have always tested new treatments and drugs."

Car says, "So you test The Cure knowing that you will have fatalities resulting from your decision to deny them treatment. Isn't that akin to murder?"

The Government says, "Yes. It's the way we've always done it. You have to break a few..."

I interrupt, "Don't say it! No more platitudes! We're not making an omelet here."

The Government says, "Either do it our way or hire someone else to do it for you. If you decide to hire someone else you will have to release any information they request. What do you want to do?"

I say, "We'll have the results for you in a few months. Our Board Certified Test Team will naturally comply with the certified procedures. If we hired someone else they would do it the same way anyhow, so there would be nothing gained by hiring someone else, would there?"

I turn the testing over to my Certification Team and wait for the results. It has not been long in coming.

After seven months of testing I'm surprised to find that there is a three percent higher survival rate among the people who thought they were being treated when they weren't. I guess there is such a thing as the power of faith.

The Cure had a ninety nine percent cure rate. The one percent failure was due to the person's terminal illness having done fatal and irreparable physical damage. We treated that person too late to save them. I propose having a vigil for the people who died in the trials.

Car warns me against having a vigil. He fears that it may somehow imply a wrongful death liability on our part.

I called for a period of mourning anyway. Farmer Industries held a midnight vigil for all of those who died in the testing of The Cure. Implications aside, I must do what feels right.

I realize that its unprecedented behavior, but I grieve for those who might have been saved but weren't.

The Cure is certified for use on humans, but there is now a series of clinical trials which limit the number of people who will be allowed to receive it.

The lack of availability for The Cure is creating an atmosphere of unrest among the people.

The abolition of the court system removing all hope of appeal is also creating an undercurrent of dissatisfaction with the government.

The World Government creates a fictitious segment of the population coined as "the silent majority. It quotes the silent majority whenever there is an unpopular ruling as being the will of the people."

In spite of the laws against public gatherings to protest, the undercurrent of rage is reaching a boiling point. Something has to give.

Chapter 9 The Winds of Change

It dawns on the vast majority that they are not being governed any more. They are being ruled over. Their Constitutional Republic having already been swallowed up in a new World Government, the government made a comment just prior to the abolition of the Constitution.

The Government said, "The Constitution is just a God damned piece of paper!"

With that one comment, all the rights of all the people of the North American Continent were abolished.

The government created the new World Government and the new World Currency system in preparation for The Cure and its sociological and geopolitical ramifications.

This new system would allow the government to manage the dramatic increase in the average age of citizens.

This dramatic increase in the average age of citizen would therefore increase the dependency on entitlement programs and ultimately drive the economy into bankruptcy.

In time, due to longer life expectancy, only twenty percent of the population will be contributing to the world economy. Eighty percent of the population will either be on welfare or Social Security. These programs had to go.

In the past, businesses had retirement programs that took up a lot of the strain on the economy caused by the aging population, but the retirement programs dried up.

None of the businesses are doing anything about their retiring employees any more. The burden has all shifted to the government Social Security and welfare systems.

As with any problem, there is more than one solution. While the people slept, the government devised a solution that would best suit the ruling class.

Now the ruling class rule unconditionally.

Another solution would favor the people.

People are now demonstrating in the streets. They are tired of their signs being torn down every day and burned as fuel in the cities power plants.

Needless to say, the people who are demonstrating are being arrested and jailed for treason.

There are public executions designed to snuff out the resolve of the general public.

It isn't working.

Mobs around the world are attacking every World Government symbol. The politicians are forever at risk of assassination. The world has fallen into anarchy.

So what's the answer?

The solution that most favors all of the people is called a "Democratic Socialist Technocracy."

There has been a Technocracy in the past, but there has never been a Democratic Socialist Technocracy before. It's a brand new form of government.

In the current barbarian government, leaders trouble themselves with matters of finance and turf. Leaders are measured on how well they drive matters concerning conquest.

Government boldly confronts the people rattling their proverbial sabers and shouting threats. The secrets, the lies and the betrayals forge a foundation that will be dressed in a superficial shroud of loyalty called patriotism. It is all highly emotional stuff.

Now we are striving for a Technocracy where our leaders are elected for their potential. Our leader's performance faces the metric of achievement, not of conflict resolution. A leader derives glory from discovery, not from promises of relief from taxation. A leader derives glory from innovation, not from posturing on empty promises.

A great leader brings improvement to the lives of the people, and a higher quality of life. That is where the people want their government to go.

So a war is waged to convert the oppressive government to a brand new Democratic Socialist Technocracy.

It's interesting that this all came about because of a small invention called The Cure.

The geopolitical and socioeconomic crisis is all being driven by the increase in the average age of the population.

If science and technology are driving all the changes in our lifestyles, shouldn't the government be driven by the same forces?

This whole upside down and inside out mess is being driven by a battle between the people and the new World Government to recover people's right to be well.

In preparation for nationalization of the medical, pharmaceutical and health insurance industries, the World Government orders that every World Citizen must buy health insurance. In this way, when the World Government takes over, they will have a guaranteed medical tax in the form of insurance premiums to support their public medical system.

This is the how and why of our mandatory health insurance system.

The National Health Insurance Commission creates rules that maximize the cost of insurance.

Meanwhile, the National Medical Commission creates rules that minimize their cost and maximize our co-pay requirements.

Meanwhile, the National Pharmaceutical Commission creates rules that maximize our cost.

It costs the government ten credits for a pill (ten cents in dollar value) and the pill is priced at 1000 credits (ten dollars in dollar value).

The government doesn't actually pay the 1000 credits. Nobody does, but it justifies the citizen paying their copay of 300 credits per pill, which nets the government 300 credits minus their 10 credit cost, or 290 credits in profit per pill.

You pay, or you either die or suffer from the disease.

The government makes a handsome profit of 2,900 percent per pill.

With inflation as a factor, it's a gradual process that ever so slowly tightens the noose around the financial necks of the people.

Now, with the advent of The Cure, the National Pharmaceutical Commission will be losing trillions of credits per week.

The plan is to get mandatory cure insurance imposed on the people. This will offset the losses due to fewer prescription sales.

The next step is logical. By nationalizing the insurance industry, the government can apply the mandatory Health Insurance premiums together with the mandatory Cure Insurance premiums and double their sales.

By "managing (limiting)" the care of citizens, the government can offset the losses caused by the aging population.

If The Cure is approved for humans, there will be a high cost associated with its implementation. The burden will be on the people to financially compensate the government for the increased cost of people living longer.

If The Cure is never approved for humans, that's all the better. The government will still be reaping huge profits from the cost of medication and treatment copays.

The people are naturally becoming increasingly outraged.

Public executions are only inflaming the situation.

Americans have been the most outspoken.

Although Americans have never had a Democracy, they have had a Constitutional Republic. Now they have nothing.

President Abraham Lincoln was defeated in the election and only had 40 percent of the popular vote. The Electoral College put him in office against the will of the people.

It's just one example of how governments run roughshod over the people.

The people of America were outraged then. Now all the people of the world are totally ballistic.

I am no different.

Something must be done, and quickly.

I have not brought the world so closely to a utopian way of life just to have a group of greedy bastards in power steal it all for themselves.

Farmer Industries is the perfect organization to bring about the winds of change.

In order to do this I established meetings with the criminal underground.

The criminal underground has suffered immeasurably from the new currency. It has become virtually impossible to launder money. Drug transactions have to be funneled through legitimate banking institutions.

Large sums of money in block transactions raise flags with the government. The criminal underground is suffering. I offer them a way to eliminate the World Government.

We decide to create a segmented strategy.

The Earth would be divided up into what we call "hot spots" and "cold Spots."

The freedom fighters would be divided up into "live action" and "deferred action."

The definitions provided by segmentation provide the need for isolated identity.

Whether or not anything goes wrong, it has to be impossible to determine the source of the attack.

Robert Stetson

If the origin of the attack on the World Government can't be clearly defined, then the ability to strike back is eliminated.

In the world of changing governments there are only two kinds of resistance. There is the freedom fighter and there is the terrorist.

As to which one you are, that is decided according to which side of the battle wins. The difference between patriot and terrorist will be defined by the victor in their history books.

Our resistance movement consists of Farmer Industries as the brains and the criminal underground as the brawn.

The judicious use of robots will increase our ability to function in extreme conditions.

We use robots, but never androids.

We'll need a means to isolate ownership so they won't be traced back to us.

A joint development program is created between the criminal underworld and our manufacturing facility.

We establish secret manufacturing centers in Africa and South America to make non-humanoid robots with standard solid state electronics.

We never use 3D Chipsets in any military application against the World Government. It would tip off the government to the source.

Also we never use any android technology for this purpose either. We use non-Farmer Industries robot technology.

In a meeting located in Nigeria, we work out the requirements for successfully penetrating the enemy fortifications.

I am there with Joe the Bull, head of the Mafia.

I tell Joe the Bull, "We need a group of special forces to work in the close quarters fight for freedom in unfriendly territories."

Joe firmly vows, "We will provide the troops if you can create a training camp where they can become proficient in the tactics needed to complete their missions and make a successful exit."

I tell Joe, "We will provide a training camp deep in the outback of Australia and another deep in the Amazon in Western Brazil. How soon can you get the soldiers we need?"

Joe the Bull looks the part of a Mafia Boss. He sits there with his big Cuban cigar and his brow furrows.

Joe says, "Give me three months to get the boys together. We can provide all the weapons you need."

This partnership is going to be more difficult than I thought. I shake my head and bury it in my hands.

"Joe," I shout, "We're not doing things that way.

"You don't conquer a nation with drive by shootings. This isn't a rival gang. Things have to be done quietly."

Joe says, "Sounds like were going to have to kick ass in order to get their attention, don't you think?"

I ease back in my chair and speak, "We can kick ass for sure, but why expose ourselves to losses?

"We can hit them where it hurts and not have to fight them nose to nose if we do it right. That's what the training camp is all about. We're not going to run and jump and climb.

"Your people will spend almost all of their time in classrooms learning how to deliver the punch quietly."

Joe is getting agitated. I can tell because the cloud of cigar smoke is getting thicker.

He has had to wave his bodyguards off more than once when I spoke to Joe in a sharp tone. People who disrespect the Mafia Boss tend to disappear.

I am Joe's only hope of getting his organization back on the road to profitability. He knows this and treats me as an equal, for now.

I'm aware that Joe is like a hungry animal. You can work with him until he doesn't need you any more, then you become fair game.

For now we operate on the time honored rule, "the enemy of my enemy is my friend." Joe and I want each other dead. We want the World Government even more. We want the World Government gone badly enough that we are willing to partner in the effort. Unless we work together nothing will change.

Farmer Industries travels deep into the uncharted areas of the Brazilian forest.

We also travel deep into the unclaimed areas of the Australian Outback.

Next, we fly in construction supplies to the Outback location. We also move construction supplies to our location in the Amazon by boat.

Food and other supplies are air dropped to both locations.

After two months we have both camps completed and fully equipped. They are both camouflaged so they can't be seen from the air or by satellite.

We advertised for Special Forces Trainers and considered the best way to use them without becoming a target for the World Government.

We hired them to train what we passed off as our security people. The training is done at Farmer Industries in the United States while the camps are being constructed in Australia and Africa.

After they train our people, our people will become the trainers for the Mafia Soldiers at our secret facilities.

The construction of bombs and timers fall under the charter of the Mafia Munitions People.

The Mafia provides trainers for our secret facilities who can train everyone on the science of bombs and timers. I want everyone trained in every aspect of the missions that will be executed by the Patriot Army we're assembling.

I hired a couple of "second story" men who are experts at getting inside of difficult places, which any ordinary person could never penetrate.

"Moose" is built like a tank, but nimble. His small brown eyes are set close together and with his shaven head he looks almost cartoon like. He dresses in denim overalls and wears loafers.

Moose is accomplished in the martial arts and won the hammer throw competition in the last Olympics at Warsaw. Martial Arts and Hammer Throw expertise is an odd combination of skills for a man to possess.

Martial arts require lightning reflexes and gymnastic balance and the hammer throw requires bruit strength. Huge muscular men are generally thought of as being stupid and a bit slow of wit. I would pit Ramsey and Moose against anyone.

"Mouse" is a small wiry little guy with big black glasses. He reminds me of a skinny owl because his glasses make his eyes look huge.

If you want to break into anything, the Mouse is your man. This is true whether it's a secure military base, a secure network, or a secure computer. Mouse has a brain and the fingers to crack anything. He is also quite a gymnast.

The Mouse can scale a wall, rock ledge or anything vertical like a monkey. It's obvious from the outset that Moose and Mouse are inseparable. You have to wonder what they have in common.

The surprising truth is that they both love Opera, Ballet and according to them, gourmet Chinese food (is there is such a thing?).

Moose and Mouse have agreed to teach everything they know about infiltration to the folks in our training centers. Seems they have been out of work ever since the monetary system changed.

The World Government monitors everything. We have a rule regarding communication that no one is allowed to conduct secret business over the phone or by radio.

We don't use the Internet for sending secret Emails and we don't use the World Mail System for mailing letters or documents. Neither do we FAX.

I am in a meeting located in Zurich, Switzerland; Farmer Industries and the Mafia are settling on the rules for exchanging information.

I am there with Joe the Bull, head of the Mafia.

I tell Joe the Bull, "We need a group of couriers who are willing to travel in unfriendly territories.

I am constructing war rooms located in each of the two secret facilities. We will have to travel between them as needed.

I have private company transportation linking us to local tour companies owned by Farmer Industries. We can get you and your people in and out of both secret facilities without being noticed."

Joe firmly says, "Let's be honest here. I don't trust you. You don't trust me. We each need our own couriers. My boys will deliver my messages for me. Who are you going to get?"

I tell Joe, "Don't worry about me. I'll work it out. Just make sure we have couriers moving back and forth every day.

By the way, Joe, I need your experts located at the secret facilities to work the weapons and explosives. I am going to set up a manufacturing facility on site there to provide robot construction.

Joe asks, "Why there?"

I respond with, "Because we need to keep every aspect of the operation under wraps. If we have several locations involved in an operation, they will have to transport incriminating materials back and forth. Having everything in one secret facility means we only ever have to move anything we use once."

The meeting is then adjourned.

I call a meeting of Farmer Industries Senior Staff and we are doing a risk analysis with regard to the courier issue.

Turning first to my VP of Security I ask, "What are the pros and cons of using people or androids as couriers?"

The VP of Security says, "Humans are not usually the best security risk because they tend to have their own loyalties and ambitions.

"Androids have no personal or loyalty issues.

"Humans will need the message in some form of media, such as paper or film.

"An android is like a computer and can store the secret messages and images in their memory.

"I favor the android if you can make them look and act like real people."

My Manufacturing VP says, "I can groom them to be tourists and give those androids with unique racial appearances varying nationalities and language skills.

"Each of them will be bilingual. For example, The Japanese android will speak and understand both English and Japanese."

I say, "This is perfect. How soon can we have them ready to travel?"

My Manufacturing VP says, "I can have them ready to travel in about two weeks."

I smile and say, "Do it."

Moving the building supplies and equipment into the secret facility locations is tricky, but by using a variety of paths for moving building supplies.

To an observer it would look as though we are doing home improvements because the material is purchased in a variety of outlets and moves in small batches.

We could have the whole thing done in a month, but we're pacing our material delivery slowly enough so as to not generate suspicion.

Our tour company in Brazil is called Brazilian River Tours. Our tour company in Switzerland is called Snow Time Tours.

Our first mission is to monitor the World Government satellites, radio and telephone communications. Our second mission is to disrupt that same communication medium and be able to inject our own messages in the stream.

Moose and Mouse go to work on our systems to map the World Government repeaters. Later we can hack into their computers and tap their satellite links.

Mouse is working around the clock writing lines of code to decipher and collect information based on its relevance to our missions.

When each computer program is completed and tested, one of our android couriers stores the program in their memory, and then travels to the other secret facility to install it.

Since travel is always aboard our company transportation systems, security is never an issue and our couriers are never subjected to airport or harbor transportation screening.

In today's political situation, we become the intruder and we find ourselves in the domain of the established World Government.

We are doing some laborious work to narrow our options.

We decide that we can't eliminate the information problem by spying. The best we can do is monitor their communications and activities to some extent. The extent to which it becomes possible is dependent on just how far we're ready to go in accomplishing that task.

We come up with a plan, and it looks like it will easily work.

We're going to need some special talent to pull it off, and the talent we need isn't the talent we have on hand, so we make a call to our newly found contacts in the criminal world and request two special second story men be dispatched ASAP to work with Moose and Mouse along with a Communications Engineer and a Com-Link Installer.

It's more difficult to run a stealth operation when you start amassing large numbers of people. If this operation is to succeed we have to keep our numbers to a minimum.

Already the World Government patrols have increased in their frequency since we arrived.

Our team of four specialists finally arrives. As they step out onto the platform I recognize them from the photos in my hand.

The Communications Engineer is a short guy with a wiry mustache.

The Com-ink Installer has his equipment with him in the form of a small silver case. I wince and think they might as well have embroidered "Com Link Installer" on his shirt.

The two second story men have arrived as well and are called "Cotton" and "Breeze." I could never get over how operatives always seem to pick up nick names. The nick names are always alluding to their special abilities.

I'm told that Cotton can move through an area, clean out all the valuables and not rouse any watch dogs.

Breeze is said to be able to break into places that appear impenetrable. The smallest crack in your security and you will feel the breeze.

We gather yet one more time in the conference room and go over the plan. We will only need four people aside from me.

Now we sit tight and wait for closing time over at World Hall.

Moose and Mouse are upset because we brought in Cotton and Breeze. They think they could have resolved our problem without bringing in outside help.

I take them aside and explain, "Look guys, I not only need these people. I need their special communications link equipment. It's brand new. It's very special. If we take on the equipment, we have to take on these people as well."

Moose and mouse nod in agreement.

I say, "Just tag along and if these clowns screw it up, you can bail us out."

Moose and Mouse smile and say, "We'll be standing by."

Six hours after closing time we are sure the building is empty except for their security.

We step out the front door of the office and walk over to the back entrance.

This is an ideal night for such a clandestine operation. It's almost impossible to see the stars above because the night is thickly overcast.

Robert Stetson

We go to the lower level in the Hall to the communications office. We get in the elevator and proceed to the communications room.

Once inside the elevator lobby, Cotton, Breeze and I press the button and wait while the elevator comes to our floor. The elevator arrives with a soft "ding" and the doors silently open. Moose, Mouse, Cotton, Breeze, the Communications Engineer and the Com-ink Installer are all moving by way of the elevator to the World Hall interior.

Our night vision glasses work well in the pitch darkness as we enter the World Hall building with the unlit halls and rooms. The night vision goggles work remarkable well since they have their own infra-red light source.

We don't want to turn on any white lights in the interior of the World Hall offices and alert anyone that we're in here.

As we move swiftly and quietly through the halls it's so quiet you can hear the six of us breathing.

Cotton goes straight to the World Government Investigative offices without delay.

He taps into the computers, puts his one hundred terabyte memory stick in the port and copies all of the files pertaining to the operations of the monitored companies.

There is a new folder called "Farmer Industries". Cotton copies that one to our memory stick and erases most of those files on the main computer.

Cotton calls up the archives, which are always kept alive and on line in case they're needed.

He does a global search for the words "Gill Bennett" and deletes the backup files as well. Then he takes his memory stick out of the computer, puts it in his pocket.

Now for the most important part of our mission here, we plant the evidence that will hamper their efforts to interfere.

We plant a message in their outgoing database and leave it unencrypted for everyone to read. The message says, "Gill Bennett is no longer a person of interest".

Cotton smiles and makes a series of clucking sounds, then says, "Making sure the World Government Security Monitors take a copy. This couldn't get more clear is we posted runway lights."

On the way out the door, Cotton artfully cleans any fingerprints.

Breeze, the Communications Engineer and the Com-Link Installer are all busy in the basement of City Hall. They are working in the communications utility room where they have located the eight broadband feeds to the World Government Investigator's office on the floor above.

The Com-Link Installer pulls out a special tool and injects a micro transmitter under the insulation of each feed link cable at a point just before the information is encoded, giving us a clear and unencrypted data stream.

These eight special transmitters will then encode the information for us just before transmitting to us. The Communications Engineer tests each of the transmitters as it is installed.

Since the low power transmitters have such a weak transmission signal, they will remain undetected. They get their micro power from the signal they're monitoring so they can work for several years without a failure.

We are finding the information flow to be so voluminous as to require all eight channels to be monitored by computer parsing monitors.

These micro transmissions are monitored at our two war rooms, one in Brazil and the other in Switzerland. By filtering the data stream for relevant information before forwarding it to the war rooms, we cut the volume to no more than a mere twenty percent.

Subsequent monitoring has determined that the World Government has no idea where the training camps are located.

As for the taps we have planted in the World Government communication lines, we are not only monitoring the data stream, but we are injecting messages that confuse and confound the operation.

As we plant these messages, the World Government National Security

Police are scrambled to attack and shut down various locations; many of them are World Government operations.

We are keeping the National Security Police hopping with phony messages.

I asked if there was anything else of interest in the data stream.

Cotton says, "Did you know there are government owned farms for meat, dairy products and produce?" Cotton pulls a block of data and puts the conversation on the monitor screen. It was a head shot of a man speaking with the seal of the World Government behind him on the wall. This message is interdepartmental and not intended to be seen by the general public.

He says, "We have to protect our critical Government Leaders. In the event of a national emergency, the World Government Leaders will have their own captive food supplies."

With everything in place we go to Brazil and settle into the War Room to play with the eight channels of filtered information that's streaming in over the satellite data lines.

By now Moose, Mouse, Cotton, and Breeze are the best of friends and have their heads together.

Every time I hear them chuckle I know we hurt the World Government again.

They are working so well I just stay out of their way and let them do their thing.

I can't quite contain myself and say, "You boys play nice now."

I'm watching the evening news on the War Room TV screen and there it is!

The announcer is running the captured internal video from the World Government with the spokesman saying, "We have to protect our critical Government Leaders. In the event of a national emergency, the World Government Leaders will have their own captive food supplies."

There are riots in the street. The World Government Building is under siege by angry mobs as we continue to cross the feeds between the World

Government and the news network satellites.

The Government never knows where information is going and the news media never knows where the information is coming from.

It's time to consider that with victory so close, the criminal underground will be a problem.

It's also time to professionalize our approach to establish a new World Government. We need to put up a front as a highly credible replacement for the current establishment.

We selectively offer secret cure treatments to people high up in the resistance movements around the world.

We don't just cure them and their relatives and friends; we use the treatment centers to indoctrinate the other resistance groups into our movement. It ensures that we will control the government after the fall, which is closer with every passing day.

I don't want our partners, the criminal underground; in the picture when it's time to establish our new government.

Our data team goes to work injecting information into the World Government's data network.

We are giving up every known criminal's location and identifying them as the cause of the World Government's demise.

The VP of Finance jumps up and shouts, "We are becoming worse than the World Government"

We don't stop until every available criminal has been converted to the fate of a Goon. The Government is retraining the Criminal Goons in various disciplines, from heavy labor to factory workers, to roughnecks, and then to suicide soldiers in a desperate attempt to stop the rioting mobs.

With the World Government on the run, I introduce myself as the new candidate in the upcoming Constitutional Republican Technocracy.

Nancy and I have our remaining clones standing by to impersonate us in

Robert Stetson

upcoming appearances.

Things are still a bit too volatile for Nancy and me to show our faces in front of a crowd. Until we stabilize the political situation, the world will be looking at nothing but android clones. Assassination attempts on my life are bound to happen.

The political scene splits into two groups of contenders for the new World Government.

There is the group suggesting Democracy as a new method of governing. In a Democracy with ninety plus percentage of the world being in poverty, the poor will rule the Earth.

There is the group suggesting A Republic as a new method of governing. In a Republican Government with less than one percent of the world being wealthy, and the rules established by a litany of edicts, the rich will rule the Earth.

The Democratic Technocracy has established a method of voting that will guarantee majority rule at the poles.

The Constitutional Republican camp has established a method of maintaining control of the government by establishing Electoral Collages to select and elect candidates without regard to popular opinion.

The most popular among the world citizens is the Democratic method of government, so the Republican camp had a problem, but not for long.

The Constitutional Republicans came up with an easy compromise.

The Constitutional Republicans promise a majority rule at the poles. They even make it a point to tout all their efforts to monitor and police the security at the poles and ensure that voter tampering won't be an issue.

Then they establish an Electoral College to select and elect candidates without regard for popular opinion. What could be fairer?

Now the day comes, as we knew it would. The doors of the World Government come crashing down and the ruling class is ejected from their thrones.

There is a vacancy in the halls of the World Government.

The world is in chaos.

We step up to fill the void.

Crowds clash on the steps of the World Capital.

Our Democratic android Goons step in with their new and highly attractive World Police uniforms and quiet the raging mobs.

With control of the news feeds, we are able to convince the people of Earth that our government is in place and is favored by a majority of the world citizenry.

There will be no Constitutional Republic. There will be a new world order in the form of a Democratic Technocracy.

We use the manipulation of the news feeds to convince the world that the only stable government would have to be a technocracy. In the past leaders troubled themselves with matters of finance and turf. Leaders were measured on how well they drove matters concerning war.

Governments would boldly confront each other rattling their proverbial sabers and shouting threats. The secrets, the lies and the betrayals forged a foundation that would be dressed in a superficial shroud of loyalty called patriotism. It was all highly emotional stuff.

Now we have a Technocracy where leaders are elected for their potential. Our leader's performance faces the metric of achievement, not of conflict resolution.

A leader derives glory from discovery, not from promises of relief from taxation. A leader derives glory from innovation, not from posturing on empty promises surrounding legislation.

A great leader brings improvement to the lives of the people and a higher quality of life.

Over the next few months there are several attempts on my life.

The android lookalikes are taking a beating from the losers in the race to take over the world throne.

The next question I have to answer is what direction I would like to take with regard to my life. Do I want to be a world leader, or do I want to run the factory and continue to create new solutions? The decision is difficult to arrive at. Can a leader do both?

Nancy and I talk endlessly about the benefits of each career path and decide that we might be better off working to make The Cure accessible to the people of the world.

With Kevin pretty much under control and the criminal underground essentially eliminated, there is little left to deter us from our goal.

Nancy and I are now more tired than ever from all the hard work that a political campaign can require. Once again I just want to whisk her away on a second honeymoon in Rome.

Just as before, I want the honeymoon trip to Rome to be a surprise. I have our travel office arrange the trip. Our company jumbo jet will have to be prepped for the trip and winter is setting in. I have our trip scheduled for late spring just as before so she can enjoy the flowers and sidewalk cafes.

Nancy being Nancy, she is usually on top of everything that goes on because more than ever she is my business partner.

This time Nancy doesn't find out.

For now I have a much larger problem. If I'm not to be the world ruler, then who would I put in my place?

The answer becomes obvious. Nancy would be the perfect choice, but she is not a technologist. My spirits sag at the realization that she would never be elected.

Another problem is that people would want to see her birth certificate which was lost soon after her village was burned.

I ask Nancy, "Honey, if you had a choice of who to have in the World Government as our leader, who would that be?"

Nancy doesn't skip a beat, but answers, "Make an android and train him to be our new World Leader.

It will give you some control over the legislation while ensuring that the government doesn't turn into a runaway graft machine."

Realizing that the higher you go in government, the easier it is to call the shots; I am amazed at her insight.

I ask, "Isn't it time we had a woman leader?"

Nancy smiles and says, "Yes, homey, but we can make that our next project. For now we need to make it a man so it's easier to get him into office. People aren't that advanced in their thinking quite yet."

Creating my world leader android wasn't as difficult as I had thought. It turns out that a politician isn't as complicated as they seem to appear when they're addressing us.

The motives are clear and the objectives are clear. Just draw an imaginary logical line between what you want to accomplish and what you have to say to accomplish it. You will get what you want and your home free.

Farmer Industries manufactures thirty androids having handsome features and grey temples. The android is made to look like an executive. The androids are dressed in the finest silk suits and patent leather shoes.

Now Nancy is saying, "Gill, maybe it's time to change the name of Farmer Industries to something else.

"What do you think?"

It never occurred to me to change the name, but it sounds like a good idea to me.

I say, "Yes, my love. It sounds like a great idea. Can't help but wonder why it never occurred to me."

Nancy says, "I like the name Bennett Manufacturing. What do you think?"

I answer with, "Let's get right on it after the election. Right now we're not going to have time to do much else."

We name the World Leader android Derik Stone and present him to the world as an accomplished engineering Ph.D.

We flood the news feeds with remarkable accomplishments, most of which never happened.

The public is impressed.

Ultimately we manage to get his name on the ballet and Derik Stone is elected by a landslide.

The opposition is asking to see his birth certificate. I knew this would be a problem. The press just keeps changing the subject and downplaying the importance of the document.

People's faith in the accuracy of the news has proven once again that if the news is behind you are sure to win.

The title of the new World Leader is "Lord Eminence".

He is referred to as "His Lord Eminence"

His name becomes "Lord Eminence Stone"

Nancy and I go to work on the company name change and soon it's officially named "Bennett Manufacturing".

I had no idea how expensive it is to change the name of a company. There is more involved than new business cards and stationary. A new logo and branding have to be created.

It takes a month to get everything done, but I'm glad we did it. Now the company really feels as though it belongs to me.

Chapter 10 Brave New World

With Lord Eminence Stone in the "World House" Gill's reputation and credentials are rescued by decree.

Gill has acquired titles and degrees to the point where it seems pointless. Gill has become Heir Doctor Professor Bennett, Sir Gilbert Bennett, His Honor Bennett, Gill Bennett Esquire and every other kind of Bennett and/or Gill Bennett you can imagine.

People around the world are living to be one hundred and forty years old or more.

It was discovered that the mitochondria can be replaced to reawaken the body's ability to renew its energy. The condition is called mitochondrial disease.

Also when cells divide, the telomeres (DNA that form end-caps for the DNA's helix) get shorter. Eventually the telomeres are so short the cell can no longer divide.

Bennett's Labs have found a way to renew and replace these defective cell components.

I have become a celebrity with speaking engagements being offered in such numbers that I have to agonize over which ones would be the most beneficial to the world.

Then Nancy comes to the rescue again with another idea.

She says, "Why not prepare your speeches and have your android doubles deliver the talks.

No one would know it isn't you. You can make twenty times the money and think of all the good you could do out there."

I stop and ponder the idea for a while and say, "Won't people wonder how I manage to appear in twenty different locations at the same time?"

Nancy just smiles that cute little smile she does so well.

Then I say, "Everywhere I go, people crowd around and ask for my autograph. If you can't tell the automated autograph from the original autograph, is it really collectible?"

Nancy says, "Is it your responsibility to preserve the market value of your signature?"

I mutter, "I wish we had more answers and fewer questions."

Nancy says, "Gill, isn't it you who says that knowing the right question is often more important than having the right answer?"

She always seems to win every debate. It's most embarrassing that she does it using my own words.

With The Cure being a new tool in the war on disease, the world is changing more than anyone ever anticipated.

The median average age of the people has risen to one hundred and three.

Only one in seven people are working. The rest are retired.

The government has continued to increase the retirement age every few years, but it hasn't kept pace with the balance between the number of people contributing to Social Security and the number of people collecting.

The world and society as a whole has become a blend of retirement and welfare state.

If not for the androids working to provide goods and services, the world couldn't function.

It's been determined by sociologists that the android is a natural product of evolution. They enable people to live out an extended life and still maintain their hierarchy of needs.

Now the androids provide food, shelter and clothing to the masses. They build and maintain our cities, farm our foods, maintain order and more.

There is no gold or silver standard associated with currency. Those foundations were abandoned in the nineteenth century when the dollar went from the "silver certificate" having value based on gold and silver held in trust, and changed to the "Federal Reserve Note" which amounts to an IOU slip. The "Federal Reserve Note" is much like Wimpy in the Popeye cartoons saying I'll pay you tomorrow for a hamburger today.

There are but three occupations left in the world. One is an entrepreneur, another is a welfare recipient, and the third is a retiree.

There are but two classes of people in the world, one is the worker who does so voluntarily, and the other enjoys a career of recreation.

There is no crime because there is nothing to steal.

There is no challenge because there is nothing you have to fix to improve your condition.

There is no reason to study because you have nothing to strive for.

There is almost no reason to live, and life has become so long.

The day has arrived for Nancy and me to embark on our second honeymoon.

I break the news to her about our trip to Rome, at last.

She is excited and rushes right out to shop for a whole new wardrobe for the trip.

It's no bother. We are so rich we can't possibly spend all of our money. In fact, the money accumulates so fast we can't even spend it as fast as it grows.

Our romance is about all I have left that I could possibly lose. Nancy seems so in love with me and I am more in love with her than I have ever been with anyone.

The time comes to leave for Rome and our android staff has done everything we need done.

The ride to the airport is smooth. We are enjoying the trip more than ever because the car is a convertible. No one is out to kill us anymore.

The airport is busy, but our company airplane is parked and warming up for the trip.

As we walk out onto the tarmac, Nancy turns and crosses behind the tractor that is backing up to tow the airplane away from the gate.

Her attention is on me while the tractor driver is looking up to align his vehicle with the airplane body.

Neither of them see that she is about to be crushed between the connecting tow bar and the front landing gear.

There is a crunch and Nancy is caught between them.

I call out to her, "Nancy! Oh my God! Honey! Are you alright? Please, be alright."

Nancy makes no sound as she is mangled between the tow truck and the airplane.

She emitted a spark and a curl of smoke.

Nancy is missing a leg and her arm is crushed along with her torso, but there is no blood.

Her torso is split wide open and the inner mechanism is open to our view.

I am hoping that this is one of the duplicates I had the factory make for me and that this wreckage is somehow here by mistake and is not Nancy.

The first phase of mourning is denial. I am feeling denial right now and the hope that she is alive and well.

Maybe the real Nancy is back there at the office.

This android has a vacant look in the eyes.

I can see that it is not the human wife I married, but just an android that came by mistake.

I have never felt so all alone. I am surrounded by androids here at the airport. There is no human to tell my feelings to.

There are so many memories.

All the clues that came along, revealing themselves to me one after the other.

She knew in advance that I was going to propose.

She knew immediately that I was planning this trip.

She went into combat mode when our wedding was attacked picking me up bodily and stuffing me into the limo while firing a machine gun with deadly accuracy with the other free hand.

The company always knew where we were when we were abducted. That was obviously based on her uplinked GPS readings.

She communicated with the other androids by satellite link even while she was tied and gaged, guiding them to our location. There were so many clues.

I was so blinded by love that I never saw what was right under my nose.

I cancel my trip to Rome and return to my office. Without Nancy there doesn't seem to be any point in going to Rome alone.

I am grieving the loss of my life partner.

My feelings are reeling because I know that I never had a life partner. I just thought I did.

This complicates things dramatically because Nancy was an integral part of the business and she will be missed by everyone who works with us.

Now she will be perceived as missing.

If there is an investigation I will be a murder suspect.

I will need to think.

Members of the company who were here before me tell me they knew Nancy was an android, but either decided not to tell me, or thought I knew it already.

Kevin Farmer had her manufactured by the Escort Factory to serve as his sex slave. He had her made to also serve as his administrative assistant.

She was programmed with all the bells and whistles that would make her an executive in the company and be his lover whenever he needed one.

Kevin gave her to me so she could watch me and report back to him.

He was counting on my not realizing that she was an android.

Her expert lovemaking and her winning personality would allow me to share everything with her.

She was the perfect mole.

He didn't count on being removed from the company, but when he heard she and I were going to be married he must have had one hell of a laugh.

The whole thing, the wedding, the marriage, all became his private joke.

He wanted revenge for all I had done to him and he just got it in spades.

I sit for hours trying to figure out what the hell all of this has meant.

She seemed so sincere when she gave me love. The tenderness was so real.

Did she feel anything for me or was she responding because she knew that it was what I needed?

Was the passion the meaningless passion of a whore, or a machine merely fulfilling the function it was designed to perform?

I am feeling so empty. I am feeling so much like a fool.

I also realize that she often made remarks and offered suggestions that were not in Kevin's best interest.

It's as though over time her loyalty shifted to me alone.

Was that real?

I frequently weep openly. I frequently weep intensely. I frequently weep knowing that the pain is all about me alone.

The five stages of mourning are so hard to work through. I am well past the first stage which is denial.

Robert Stetson

The time has come to stop feeling sorry for myself and move on. Kevin has had his private joke. The joke is over.

Nancy was never the one who betrayed me. She performed her task faithfully as assigned.

I am reminded of the Kübler-Ross model, commonly known as The Five Stages of Grief in her book On Death and Dying. These stages are denial, anger, bargaining, depression, and acceptance. I think I'm at anger right now because I just want to strangle Kevin.

With everything at stake it's time to put this behind me and get back to work.

I have one of the Nancy doubles sent over just to avoid the "where is Nancy" questions.

This unit is not Nancy and I can't let her answer any questions because the programming and intelligence are not there.

I'm still piecing it all together and remember it was the company Doctor who signed off on the blood test. Had we gone to a regular Doctor, we would have found out back then that she wasn't human.

All the times the androids had problems freaking out and doing the funky chicken dance, Nancy was always out of town or back home. She must have been affected too, but I never got to see her programing go haywire because we were always apart when it happened.

Now I have multiple problems because the world has assigned her a Social Security Number, a Birth Certificate and a Marriage Certificate.

Nancy is legally listed as human. Even though she was a machine, she is a certified person. She can legally die.

I look over at the android sitting on the couch and say, "Just as there was no legal means to make Nancy human, there is no legal means to make her inhuman."

The android sits and stares at me like a marionette without anyone holding the strings.

I say, "If I keep my Nancy androids in the picture to prevent anyone from wondering why Nancy is missing, that will only work for a while, otherwise there will be a murder investigation and I will be the prime suspect."

The android just sits there and doesn't respond.

I say, "The Nancy androids would never age. In twenty years she will still be as young as she is today.

"Any way I slice it there is no way out of this situation."

The Nancy android speaks, "How many times did Nancy do your thinking for you?

"What's wrong with you, Gill?"

I turn and face my verbal aggressor.

I shout, "What do you know?

"Aside from the features on your face, you aren't her!

"What the hell are you talking about?"

The android just stares at me with unblinking eyes. It's nothing more than a talking doll.

Then the android says, "What if Nancy accidently dies in front of the world and there is no body left to examine?"

I am shocked at the revelation. I never thought of staging her death that way.

Perhaps murder is something I'm not capable of, even though it isn't real. How can I possibly pull this off?

People can't just call the ruler of the world on the phone at will, except for me. I put this World Leading Android in office and it will respond to my telephone call.

I pick up the phone and tell my Secretary to get me Lord Eminence Stone on the phone. It's just a matter of minutes before my phone rings.

Robert Stetson

Lord Eminence says, "Gill, is that you?"

There is a list of key words to use on contact.

I answer with the key phrase to show it's really me, "Godiva".

Lord Eminence responds, "Good to hear that, Gill. Why are you calling me?

"What can I do for you?"

I ask "Can you arrange a special lab to be assigned to me on the moon.

"I want to send Nancy to conduct a company study on the effects of weightlessness and low gravity on our android products."

Lord Eminence says, "We have a large contingency of androids on the moon. They are working well. We don't know what we would do without them. They function perfectly in the airless environment without space suits and they need no food.

"Why are you sending Nancy?"

I say, "Nancy has a degree in engineering. She will conduct the study there.

"The object of the study is to see if we can optimize the androids we send into space to function better in low or zero gravity."

Lord Eminence says, "You know I will do anything you ask, Gill. Have her go to the Florida launch facility along with anything you need to send with her."

I say, "Just one more thing, Lord Eminence. I would like to use our company shuttle to send her in.

"We can park it out of the way on the moon and it will enable us to bring her back any time we want without disrupting your missions."

Lord Eminence laughs and says, "How thoughtful. That will work fine.

"You can arrange with the launch team there and leave any time you want.

"I'm giving you top priority for the launch date and time."

I have the navigation control programmed by one of my programming androids. The moon trajectory program is altered by the programming android according to my instructions.

When the programming task is completed, I crush the 3D Chipset that is the brain of the programming android.

I throw the crushed 3D Chipset away and replace it with a new 3D Chipset. In this way there is no record of the program changes made to the shuttle.

We load up the transport that takes Nancy to the launch facility.

Our shuttle is loaded onto the gantry and moved to the launch pad.

The countdown progresses well and the ship is launched on its way to the moon.

Nancy is on her way to the moon along with a team of androids and a cargo of equipment. The entire operation is fully equipped.

The Launch Center monitors the progress of the shuttle until it gets within landing distance of the moon.

Alarms blaze and the whole mission board illuminates with red flashing lights. The screaming enunciators are silenced so we can think.

The Mission Chief says, "What is happening up there?"

One of the workers says, "The company shuttle has gone off course. It appears that it is going to slingshot rather than entering a landing trajectory."

I shout, "No!"

The ship whips around the moon picking up speed and goes out the other side of the moon where it heads in toward the center of the solar system and vanishes into the sun where it's vaporized.

Nancy is lost forever.

I leave the facility with my hands over my face. I'm aware of the micro expressions that give liars away.

I don't want a record of my facial expressions and I decline to speak.

I just sit in the back of my limousine and keep my face covered.

Over the next several weeks I am bombarded with news media wanting to talk to me about the death of my wife. I decline every time.

After returning to Bennett Manufacturing I order that all of the Nancy androids be dismantled and reconfigured as office workers with random facial features.

There is no walking likeness of Nancy.

As for me, I am working on some of the ideas that just seem to keep coming.

I ponder the contribution that The Cure has made to the world.

The median age is starting to drop again after rapidly rising almost out of control at first.

Suicides are up twelve hundred percent this year. People have no reason to live and their lives are twice as long as before.

Life without struggle is no life at all. Boredom and depression are kindred souls.

We are much like mechanical springs. Without something to press against, we serve no purpose.

We have discovered the meaning of life after all. Our joy is in the journey through life, not life itself.

--- The End ---

ABOUT THE AUTHOR

There is a starving artist inside each of us. Who hasn't wanted to write that novel?
These theories and plots come to me in dreams. In my mind there are no scientific inaccuracies in my works because the science in my fiction is factual.

Log onto my Web Site for a link to Amazon.Com special deals and for information on other books I have written;

http://WWW.RobStetson.Com

15458438R00109

Made in the USA
Charleston, SC
04 November 2012